Pr

'Don't underestimate a dangerous woman. And don't judge by appearance; evil can be pleasant and pretty on the outside. Just like poison candy!'

Joni E Johnston Psy.D.

Sitting on the Savannah shoreline this evening seemed fresh and freeing for me. The last couple of months have been intense, to say the least. I never would have believed killing someone would be so taxing, both mentally and physically, for a girl like me. Well, killing period! You know, at the same time, a calming and truly hypnotic ordeal overall. I guess that's how crazy works, right?

Understand I'm not trying to boast or anything, it's just that Collin killed my sister. He needed to feel the pain of what he had done. Jack and the FBI weren't going to do that. I had to be the one to do it, and I did! I really had no idea that this one act, an act of vengeance, would change the course of my life, and the lives of so many other people. But it did! I'm in no way sorry, so tonight is my night to relax and forget the past couple months.

My mission of vengeance is done, or at least I thought it was...? I found the perfect place to let go, too. Savannah, Georgia. Her streets are on fire. Tonight is the Southern Nights Jubilee, held every year at the start of Fall.

All of Savannah is dressed as if they were Southern royalty from years past. The women in their big flowery hats, fluffy hoop dresses, and their many-colored lace parasols being twirled in circles. Sipping on Mint Juleps as they strolled through the historic river district. We can't forget the men in their Southern Gentlemanly suits and walking canes, most sucking on cigars while strolling through the park. Some are even dressed as Confederate and Union soldiers with swords and civil war side arms, pretending to battle their enemies in the streets of Savannah. Others are walking their dogs and tipping their hats as they address each other as Colonel and Brigadier, how fun is this?

As I stood on my balcony at the Olde Harbor Inn, directly across from the park, smells of crawfish and hush puppies filled the air. I could see street performers of all kinds drifting in and out of the crowds. They were spreading fun amongst the people and grifting a few pockets along the way. In the meantime music was playing from every street corner, filling the void between our ears with sweet southern sounds. Such a perfect place to just disappear...

Disappearing is exactly what this girl needed to do after my little project out on Cock-spur Island this morning. The end of Collin, a "Cock-spur" of a man! That's exactly what he was too, such a fitting name and a fitting end for that piece of garbage. That horrible man got away with killing Sara and so many other innocent women, to think he would still be out there looking for his next kill, but karma is a real bitch, right...?

I popped out of my hotel and headed towards the lights near the beautiful tree lined park on East River St. The park was right next to the boardwalk on Bay Street, with cute little local shops and restaurants serving the most delicious southern treats ever. Tonight, tent vendors were set up on the edge of the park with alluring handmade trinkets for sale and those old carnival games no one ever wins. You know the kind, the three stacked milk bottles, skeet roll and who could forget the ring toss, but people didn't really care if they won or lost, that's not the point of those old games.

The city's people just laughed and strolled these historic paths, forgetting what problems they had encountered hours before at work and in their personal lives. They were out to forget, just like me. And all the while--- not knowing that a murderer walked amongst them tonight, what a rush this was. Yes, that was what I became, a murderer killing another murderer, but I'm not sorry. This celebration was my therapy, I avenged my sister, and now I'm at peace, right?

You would think so, that had been the plan. I simply kill him and get back to my life in New Orleans, easy, right? But I can't figure out why there is still a gnawing in my head and this anxiety in my stomach. Where is the peace? I just killed a serial killer who deserved it after all. I should be the hero, right? Well at least my sister, Sara, can rest in peace now!

If you asked my therapist, Mary, back home in New Orleans, what was wrong with me, and why I had murdered someone, I'm sure she would just fall out of her big orange therapy chair, and choke on her stupid Italian biscuits that she ate at every session. I couldn't blame her though; I never told Mary that I was planning to kill Collin. I guess---I missed that session. Don't get me wrong, she's great. Since I moved to New Orleans after college to start my life, she has helped me walk through many challenges in these recent years.

Mary and I worked on issues like the loneliness of having no family, no one anywhere, not even a cat. That whole, very select friends' thing, which has plagued me since childhood, right? We don't want to forget the over-achieving problem at school, at work and at life in general. Or my favorite, the OCD and ADHD challenges that make me who I am today, at least according to Mary.

Mary is good at the normal crazy stuff of life. Me killing my sister's killer is just past normal crazy --- in most psychological play books anyway. I'm sure she would go into an Italian biscuit overload with this one. I'm also sure Mary will be asked at some point by the police if she thought I was capable of killing someone---is anyone really capable of murder? A question I now know the answer to.

I guess sometimes life has a different plan. In the end of this adventure---my adventure of vengeance---you will have to be the judge and the jury of my actions, deciding whether I have done wrong, or whether you believe it's justice for the innocent.

Chapter 1

The End to the Beginning

'No trait is more justified than revenge in the right time and place.'

Meir Kahane

Morning came; I was still sitting on the floor of the hotel bathroom in my robe thinking about what was really going to happen today. The plan, the plan is today, my plan... It's happening today, today is now... Everything that I have been working toward all these months is about to come true.

Through the small crack in the doorway, I could see Collin spread naked across the bed still sleeping. As I looked at him, it's hard to believe I let him have me, after what I know about him and what he did to Sara, and all the other women. The reality is, last night I took him, I'm in control of the bastard now, after all, that was his last night on earth...

Dawn was about to break, that time between dark and light. It's a time of quiet peace---I love to watch as the sky begins to turn to light---it's my favorite time of the day. Today---I needed coffee!

I made my way out of the door without waking him, and to the glass elevator that overlooks the entire lobby and the office complex next door. I stood in the middle, glass all around me giving me an open look out over everything; it was like the Mall at closing time, cold and barren, a ghost town of sorts. That's what came to mind as the elevator descended to the lobby. I closed my eyes just as the ride came to an end. I prayed they had coffee ready---it was about five thirty or so.

As the doors to the elevator opened, the aroma of coffee filled the glass tube. I followed the smells, which brought me to a whole room of coffee and fixings. "HEAVEN," I said out loud. I grabbed a cup, poured the hot black liquid in and hugged its warmth. I walked over to a dark corner overlooking the lake outside; there I lost myself in the plan of events for the day. It wasn't too late to forget the plan and run back home to New Orleans.

Then I saw him, his reflection in the glass, he had spotted me in the corner as I looked out the window. He made his way over and kissed me on the back of my neck, then said he would be back in minute, coffee was in order.

I about threw up all over that window when his lips touched my neck. I knew then, the plan was on---you don't know how hard it's been to let him, a murderer, touch me. The reality is---I did fuck him last night, but I did the fucking and I had to fight really hard to not get sick all over him---after I got off, of course... How it got that far, I don't know or understand. I never could have slept with him there either. How could I close my eyes next to a killer, could you?

We finished our coffee and headed up to the room to pack and hit the door for our fun day out on Cock-Spur Island. I just love that name, right...

He thinks we are biking and picnicking out there, then heading down to Charleston. I know that's where I'm headed tomorrow, but Collin, not so much.

I chose the yellow dress and white Converse tennies, and a nice white floppy hat, from my own Jackie collection. Jacqueline Kennedy and Audrey Hepburn have been my fashion inspiration lately, all that sixties stuff, elegant and crisp. I almost forgot the most important item of all, my white gloves with the special little pouch I sewed in the palm for the Devil's Breath. A very important detail you know.

All packed, we headed down to the lobby to check out. I walked ahead of Collin, pulling the flap of my hat down while slipping out the door before the front desk girl came out and free of any cameras, I'm invisible and I plan on staying that way too...

Sitting at the front door was a nice red convertible Mustang that Jean-Paul found for me and my little project. The top was down, and it had two bikes strapped to the back just as I had ordered. Collin walked out and, of course, jumped into the driver's seat, not ever looking over to me for an ok, what an ass. The air was crisp and clean smelling today--- a bit unusual for Savannah, but I took it as a sign of how this day would go, crisp and clean. I pointed to the road and off we sped to Cock-Spur Island for a picnic and bike ride, his last!

I had him park under a tree right below the only blind curve on the island. It was the big bend in the road I had picked out earlier while doing my research of the island for the event. My God, it sounded like I was planning a party or something, that's a bit creepy. Oh hell, it'd been fun, and I knew it...

We unloaded the bikes and walked them up to the road for the ride. Collin wasn't a bike kind of guy in any way, but he was making an effort to go along with me---after last night he had better. I still can't believe I actually let him put his hands on me, gutsy---but I did and we fucked for a couple of hours before he passed out under me---I must have been a good fuck. I can't say I felt a thing, other than disgust and hatred---I think that's what got me off...

We stood at the tip of the hill just at the blind curve, straddling our bikes and talking about which way to go, when out of the corner of my eye I spotted a Blue Jeep Wrangler with its top down speeding up the road. I gently unzipped the pouch and the white powder fell out into the palm of the glove, I called his name, then leaned forward and blew the devils breath into Collins face as if I were blowing him a kiss---truth be told, it was a kiss, the kiss of death, right...?

He sniffed hard, shaking his head and choked a little, then the glaze came over his eyes, a red blush hit his cheeks, Collin was under---Collin was all mine to play with now. I was in total control. I shivered with excitement. That jeep was closer now, in range of the kill.

I leaned in and whispered in Collin's ear, "Collin, will you play with me and be a good boy---it's time for you to ride your bike. I want you to ride straight into the curve for me, and Collin---watch your feet as you pedal, it's fun."

Without any hesitation, off he went into the road and right for the on-coming jeep. He began to speed up too, right into the blind curve where the jeep full of young people was racing around at that very moment. I gripped my handlebars as he got closer and just as Collin looked up, he hit the front grill of the Jeep with the sound of metal hitting metal. I watched his body flip onto the hood, with his head smashing into the windshield, then his body rolled to left and slid head first right into the front wheel well, crushing his head like a zit... It made a popping sound as the tire rolled over it.

I watched his brain matter spit out into the road as his body flapped around under the jeep making this thumping sound. The jeep soon came to a halt. My grip tightened on the handlebars again and I let out a little gasp, as I felt myself have a tingling orgasm right there while I watched the end of Collin... Very exciting stuff, he played very well...

The poor kids, all screaming, stopped and jumped out, not noticing me standing off the side blending in with scene, I quietly rolled off down the road to the car and loaded my bike on the rack at the rear of the Mustang, and took a second to reach into Collin's bag and grab his laptop, then flipped it into my bag while looking around in all directions to make sure I was in the clear. I did take one last look up the road to see his dead, lifeless body lying in the middle of the road with no head left, just mush...

It was time to get out of Dodge, before the police got there, so I slid into the Mustang popped that baby into gear and zipped down the road back to Savannah for the night. It was my time to relax and unwind. I do believe I deserved to finally let it all go and relax, right... Tonight Savannah is having a celebration of sorts, the Southern Jubilee. The city dresses as if they were back in 1865 after the bloody war. I asked Jean-Paul to set me up in a room next to the park for the night, which he did, of course.

I made my way down the island road and over the bridge as the police and ambulance shot towards the accident. That's what they will call it, an accident. I was in the clear, with no trail leading back to me. At that moment my sister's song came over the radio as I pulled into the sand lot next to the bridge. "Playing with madness"; perfect timing for the end of my project. I listened as it played, then suddenly; I realized that without the car, there would be no trail to explain how Collin got out here.

After all, the room was in his name. I did wipe it down before we left---to erase me, but the car...

Jean-Paul put it in Collin's name, but I can't be caught in it---what to do, this is a little bit of a pickle. Thought I had everything covered, but I see I didn't---shit, I'm going to hate this next phone call, but I knew I had to, so yes, I called Jean-Paul, my secret savior of sorts. He just told me to stay put and he would send a car. He also told me to not attract any attention, and to stay in the car. I laughed and told him I was being a good girl.

Jean-Paul said his man would be there in less than ten minutes, and that he would be in a black limo. His name was Brazil, he was a short Haitian man, with a French accent. As he was finishing the sentence, I saw the limo behind me where it came to a stop. No one got out for a couple of seconds, then the door popped open and out stepped Brazil, and he was definitely short---all of four feet six maybe.

He looked around before walking over to me and introducing himself while opening my door. He gently walked me over to the limo, and as I was getting in, he grabbed my phone, snapped it in half and threw it in the water. I froze for a second not really knowing just what to think, when he handed me another phone, smiled and went back to the Mustang. Brazil took the bike off the back and walked down to the water and threw the bike in as he scanned the area for anyone watching.

After he made sure the bike sank, he grabbed my suitcase and began wiping down the Mustang for fingerprints or hair, anything that would connect me to Collin. He then joined me in the limo and asked me where I wanted to go first. I told him I had a room ready in town, and I asked him if Jean-Paul had told him where to take me?

"Yes, ma'am, he did."

"Let's just get me there, for some rest and relaxation, cool..." I replied.

"Yes, that is cool ma'am." Brazil told me that he was to stay around the hotel to make sure I was in the clear. "Is that ok, ma'am?" he said in his slow French accent.

"I'm good with that, Brazil, you can call me Raven."

"No, Ma'am, I will only address you as Miss Rousseau, that is proper." he insisted.

I slid the glass up between the front and back while I lay down in the seat and shut my eyes. The flashes of Collins head popping came first, then of Sara hanging in the tree and the image of the jogger hanging upside down from that bridge all flooded my thoughts, all at the same time. Sending me into a nice peaceful sleep, it was as if all was well and life has been put right... weird I know, but I was out like a light.

Back in the city, we pulled up to the hotel which was directly across from the river. The party was already in full swing, even though it was only one in the afternoon. These people are serious about their Jubilees now. I could smell the food and hear music all around me. Brazil grabbed my stuff and took me to the side entrance and over to the service elevator. Smart move on Jean-Paul's behalf, that gets me in under the radar, nice...

Brazil threw my suitcase on the little rack and asked if that would be all. I thanked him and said, "See you later."

"Miss Rousseau, the idea is for you not to see me, until you need me!" he said with a smile as he shut the door behind him.

I couldn't wait to jump in the shower and wash today off me; I made the water as hot as I could, kicked off my tennies, dropped my dress in the doorway and jumped in. I stood under it forever it seemed, the hot water surrounding my body, all my thoughts were of today---scene by scene right before I broke down in tears and slid to the tile floor of the shower. I had just killed a man, not directly, but killed him just the same.

My God, I planned it, I hunted him like an animal, I sacrificed myself to him, I made this all happen... I can't explain the feeling right now, yes it was wrong, I know, but who was going to make him pay for all the lives he took? Those girls he abused and killed because of his sick obsession.

Hey, I did a good thing, in a bad way, killed a killer---who would have called this one, right... I closed my eyes as the hot water rained down on me. I wanted to feel bad. I thought I should, but you know, I just couldn't. Crazy is as crazy does, right... They're free now, and as for me, I feel, well I don't really know or understand how I feel. As the hot water rained down on me while sitting naked in the corner of the shower floor, reflecting back on how all this really started...

It seemed like yesterday when I graduated from college and moved to New Orleans, worked hard at the firm putting my quiet existence together, and finally made partner at the firm. Then Sara walked into my life and everything was beginning to make sense about all the why's in both our lives. Then that Monday morning came, when the doorbell rang, and my life took that turn south... Deep, Deep South!

Chapter 2

Alligator Bayou

'Your memory is a monster; you forget---it doesn't. It simply files things away. It keeps things for you, or hides things from you---and summons them to your recall with a will of its own. You think you have a memory, but it has you!'

John Irving

My name is Raven Isabella Rousseau. RI, to the couple of people close to me, only a couple! I'm a single twenty-seven-year-old honored architect. Excited about putting a life together in my beloved hometown of New Orleans. I lived just outside the French Quarter in a house I bought right out of college. It was old and had history, something I have always been drawn to, not having any myself.

The house was my graduation present to myself, lucky me, right? The house sits near the Art District, on a tree lined street with green antique street cars passing all day long, ringing their bells and filled with tourists. Was this a picture or what...? And, of course it's close to all the historic city's action, eclectic art galleries, wild yummy southern food, and music from corner to corner. It's like my own little village. Life seemed perfect and right on track.

Then that Monday came, the day my life turned south, right into the dark shadows of the other side of life. Now, I'm being hunted by the FBI, U.S. Marshalls and the Romanian Mob---go figure, this wasn't in my life's plan at all.

As I recall, it all started the evening I made partner at the architectural firm of Mathers Brierre. They are the oldest firm in New Orleans, founded in 1891. I started there after graduating from Louisiana State University in Baton Rouge, and have been with them ever since. That was 5 years ago, how time just flies.

I really fought hard to be part of the firm. I had five separate interviews, each interview had a city river restoration project attached. It was dubbed The Waterfront Revival. I submitted letters of recommendation from my professors and finally, a visit from Professor Taylor to meet with their board, to hopefully seal the deal.

I knew I had all the credentials and awards they or any other firm, would look for, but I was young and female, not their norm. Nevertheless, for me, it was about the old, as I said before---I didn't have old in my life, so it was important for me to be part of some history, someone's history anyway, kind of like my house---it was someone's history, and now it's mine. It all worked out, I'm a young female and made partner at an all-male firm in a deep southern city...

The other partners all decided I was to take a long three-day weekend and enjoy my new position. I deserved it, they said. So here I was, having a day off, a Monday off, something I was not accustomed to in any way at all. You see, for me, being an over-achiever and workaholic, with ADHD and an ounce of OCD, days off don't compute in my brain. But, I pledged to not pick up a pencil all day...

As the morning came, I found myself down in the kitchen later than usual. I was listening to some news on the iPad while watching the water boil for my poached eggs, like I do every morning, right after my three-mile run and shower, it's my ritual. It really was kind of nice, I'll have to say.

It was almost 9:30 when my doorbell rang, startling me, sending one of the eggs to the counter, yellow yolk exploding all over the granite countertops and floor. I stood for a moment watching the yellow goop run down the front of the cabinets, trying to collect my thoughts and assessing the yolk damage, and thinking what a mess this was...

The doorbell rang again, so I hurried around the corner of the kitchen to see two figures standing at my door. In the background I could see blue and red flashing lights coming through my speckled glass door like a spinning kaleidoscope. The dancing lights bounced around my hallway, putting a smile on my face and slowed my pace a step or two after the egg yolk incident.

I swung the door open to greet the two men. Both the men were wearing blue jeans and tight tee shirts, with their badges dangling from their necks like you see on TV. I quickly studied those badges, one was smaller in size than the other and gold. It looked just like the badge Reid wears on one of my favorite TV shows, Criminal Minds.

The other badge was larger and silver, like something you would see in the Wild, Wild West. This guy had to be with the New Orleans Police Department. They have a reputation as being real cowboys, which is needed in this town of Cajun crazies. I could see their guns on their sides, not that it mattered, they just looked like bookends standing there. One of them said my name. "Raven."

I smiled, and then asked, "What's this all about, gentlemen?"

"I'm sorry, how rude, my name is Agent Jack Bode'. I'm with the FBI, and this is Detective Oliver Dupeux from the New Orleans Police Department. Can---we step in for a moment?"

"Again, what's going on here?" I repeated, with a half-smile.

"We have some questions for you about a matter we are looking into," said the FBI guy.

I looked at them, not one hundred percent ready to ask them in. I took a second and glanced over Jack's shoulder to the police car at the end of my driveway feeling a bit more at ease, but...

"Ok boys, come in." I stepped back as they entered my hall area.

"Follow me into the kitchen, gentleman. I have a mess to clean up, it's your fault by the way." I watched them glance at each other as I said that.

I grabbed the dish rag and began to wipe up the egg on the counter and front of the cabinet. I knew it would have driven me crazy if I had left it for later. That's part of the fun with my ADHD and OCD combo, clean, clean, clean, now, now, now...

"Raven, can we sit for a minute and talk about why we are here?" Jack asked.

"Sure boys, follow me to the living room, or the kitchen table, you pick?"

They both said living room at the same time, kind of cute. Jack sat next to me on the sofa with Oliver standing in front of the fireplace, holding a pad of paper and a pen in his hand ready to write. Such a stoic police thing to do, right...?

"Lived here long, ma'am?" Oliver asked in a neutral police investigative tone.

I chuckled and said, "I bought it after college." Trying to stay with simple answers for now. I wasn't sure about them yet.

"So---is that why you're here then, the house, is something wrong with the house?"

"No, Raven I wish this was that easy." Jack said.

Jack explained they had just come from Alligator Bayou where they found the body of a woman, brutally murdered. They believed her to be a friend of mine.

"Raven, do you remember Alligator Bayou? Down around Prairieville, off highway 10?" asked Jack.

Dazed I said, "Prairieville is where my parents died in a auto accident ten years ago, so yes, I do remember Prairieville," answering in a dry tone as I watched the flashing lights dance in my hallway. I was afraid of what was coming next.

Now understand, I had no friends and I just found my sister Sara two weeks ago by a fluke in events. A sister I had no idea I had. My eyes began to well up, and I could feel myself stiffen, shifting into an upright position with my hands folded tightly together in my lap. My eyes still focused on the dancing lights from the police car outside. Silence took the room, with both their eyes on me, and my reactions.

"Ma'am, are you ok?" one of them asked.

"Officer, you just told me that my sister, my sister Sara, the sister I just found after all these years, has been found brutally murdered, and you ask if I am alright? What part of this conversation is going to make me alright?"

"Sister?" Oliver looked over at Jack with a puzzled look.

Fumbling for words, as if to try and recover from the insensitive statement he had just made, Jack jumped in, "We found your name and address on the front seat of her Volkswagen Bug. It was parked in the lot at the top of the hill next to some old cabins at Alligator Bayou. The woman also had a picture of both of you hanging from her rear-view mirror. We had no idea she was your sister until now." Jack leaned in, laying the picture of Sara and I which was taken at the photo booth, on my lap.

"Her name is Sara," I said.

"Sorry, ma'am," Oliver replied quietly.

Jack reached out and touched my knee, holding his hand there, he said, "Raven, there is an old man that lives in the boathouse near there. He told us two girls from summers past were walking around the Bayou this past weekend. His name is Henry Bajoliere. Do you know him, and was that you he was talking about?"

Still watching the dancing lights, emotionless at this point, I knew I was there, but didn't want to give that up yet. I didn't fully trust them at this point. Now they know I'm connected to the Bayou because of my parent's accident, and now their case. Shit, this is not good and Sara, my Sara...

"We need you to come with us to the Bayou, Raven." Jack stated.

I looked up in shock while a wave of nausea suddenly overcame me, as they kept explaining that it would help them find out what had happened there. That I could help them understand what happened to Sara at the Bayou. Jack stood and reached out for my hand. As I placed my hand in his, a bolt of warmth shot through me; well shit, that was weird, especially, at a time like this, what did it mean? It did seem to calm me though.

As we walked to the car, all my thoughts were of Sara, hoping it wasn't her they were talking about. Jack gently sat me in the backseat of the Police cruiser and shut the door. I watched while both men stood on either side of the car, talking. I could almost hear them, I was only able to get a word or two as they talked and yes, I was the topic of the discussion. After all, they didn't know me or what to think at this point.

After about a minute they climbed in the front of the cruiser. I caught a glance from Jack's now intense blue eyes before he buckled up. *What is up with him,* I thought as we sped off,

My head was out of control at this point, not knowing if Sara was alright or why these guys wanted me to go to the crime scene. Me, at a crime scene, really, why? I just eased back and laid my head on the headrest and focused on those wooden power poles flipping by as we made our way to the Bayou. I have always loved doing that, watching those poles flip by, especially as a child on our way to the Bayou, it was kind of hypnotic.

The Bayou---the Bayou where I grew up. My parents would bring the family there every summer for years. It was a marshy arm to the mighty Mississippi. They rented a small one-bedroom cabin with a dock right off the kitchen. The cabins were on the west end of the Bayou. That's where all the family cabins were, well, four cabins that is. Each one filled with summer families like ours. Or so I thought, I would find out how untrue that really was, very soon.

Now my sister, a sister I had no idea I had, may be dead. Back then I thought she was just a summer time friend from one of the Bayou cabins. Sara had been there every summer, ready to play. Our parents would all get together for camp dinners and ping pong games. You know, all that fun family shit.

It wasn't until two weeks ago when she showed up on my doorstep, that I had any idea of the possibility of a sister, or family... You see, one long, very lonely night, while drinking a shit load of red wine, one of my weaknesses by the way, I was scrolling through Facebook, and yes, I said Facebook. I came across some survey posts about family summer fun times.

So, being a little tipsy, I wrote this two-page dissertation about my summers at Alligator Bayou. The next thing I knew, my doorbell rang one rainy Thursday night, just a week after the drunken dissertation. There my childhood friend stood, dripping wet, no umbrella in hand, just a smile.

Sara was a soaking wet mess, wearing blue jeans with holes in the knees and a Victoria's Secret tee; now totally see through from the rain, and a leather Coach Purse draped over her shoulder. What a sight she had been.

We spent the rest of that night and well into the next day in my living room on the floor, talking about what she had uncovered about us and our parents so far. At some point we had ordered veggie pizza and popped the cork on several bottles of wine, while trying to fill in what blanks we could. Trying to understand why and how all this could've happened.

The morning of the second day, I sent her to the spare bath to shower while I did the same, which gave me some time to think, to digest everything Sara was saying. My head was just spinning as I sat on the edge of the tub. Were these people really our parents or... Life had just taken a turn left into the shadows for sure.

After showering, we headed to the kitchen in our towels. We took one towel and wrapped our hair up and another towel around our bodies like a dress. It really felt like two sisters bonding. Understand I wasn't used to opening up to anybody, well---Jan my professor's wife and Mary my therapist could get me talking though. Jan used her southern drawl and her secret Cucumber Gin Smash, and for Mary, she was just fun to watch, as she tried to get me to open up, but not like this, this was a different feeling, a family feeling. I wondered if I could get used to it, I hoped so.

We had a light breakfast, poached eggs and toast, of course. All the while we kept talking, we just couldn't stop. How could we? After all, we had so much to catch up on, and pieces of our lost lives to find. Sara's life sounds as blank as mine as she tells it. But, I saw more in there though, maybe she wasn't ready to let it out yet, or me in. I didn't push too much.

Soon after we ate, we headed upstairs to find Sara some clothes to wear for our day out. As we laughed and talked, I handed her one of my sun dresses I have collected over the years. Sara slid it on while standing in front of the mirror drying her hair. I noticed Sara had a little tattoo of what looked like an arrow, twisted into an S shape.

The point of the arrow tattoo ran up her neck. The tip ended on the nape of her neck just under the end of her short black hair. I wondered what it meant. I let it go at the time, planning to bring it back up later, thinking we had a lifetime ahead of us, right...?

We jumped into her car and headed to the Courthouse on Broad Ave in the French Quarter. I had a contact from work there, who let us in and helped us check the records to see what we could find out about those people, our parents or whoever they ended up being. This is all too weird when you think about it.

We searched for hours, starting with Sara's last name, then mine, our birth years, our parent's birth years, house records, water bills, titles, school records, voting records and deeds, anything that would connect us.

By the end of the day, our efforts had led nowhere---a wasted day. Somehow there were no records of our parents or even us. Who were our parents? For that matter, who were we really?

Chapter 3

The switch flips

'A sibling may be the keeper of one's identity, the only person with the keys to one's unfettered, more fundamental self.'

Marian Sandmaier

Sunday came, and we just got lazy, watching movies and talking some more. We were very disappointed by what we didn't find at the county records office yesterday. Sara said she had a fun idea, so we jumped in her bug and took a ride down to Alligator Bayou. We wanted to walk the paths we could remember and some we didn't, anything to jog our memories at this point.

The trip down there was a top down, music filled joy ride. The day was clear, but muggy. Sara seemed to know just where to go, a left, a right---no hesitation, almost as if she had been there recently. That was my hunch anyway. Sara whipped down a dirt road and then popped into the parking lot at the top of the hill in front of the cabins. What a sight the old place was.

The cabins had that scary, weathered look from age and neglect, with strings of grey colored moss and heavy green vines engulfing them from all sides. Some of the windows were broken, and a wooden door on one of the four cabins was split in half hanging on one hinge. There were all kinds of birds floating in and out of them. A family of squirrels kept popping up all over the place and a light mist in the air helped the scary look that has taken over the place I once loved so much. Not to mention a black Crow sitting in a nearby tree screaming, that constant loud sharp, shrill of a cry that echoed through the Bayou. This place had a look right from something you would read in a Stephen King novel, like "It".

We sat in the car and talked about things we remembered from the summers we shared here. We agreed that back then, this place looked bigger. Of course it did. We were just kids then. I could see the old boathouse in the distance off to the right, and the playground and picnic area at the end of the path in front of us. The beach was still hidden behind the cypress and willow trees that seemed to wave in the breeze all day making an ominous sound. We called that area the Black Forest---it was always dark and creepy, and it hadn't changed at all. Add in the Crow and a guy with a chainsaw and you've got a perfect storm, right...?

I was rocking back and forth in my seat ready to explode inside, as If I were ten again. I needed my feet to touch the ground, to feel it, to remember it. I jumped out and Sara did the same. I sprinted to the path that led to the cabins, while Sara stood at the car watching. When I reached my old cabin, a feeling of euphoria rushed through me, my old cabin, there it was, my fortress of equilibrium.

That was my only big word as a kid, but it was true. I stepped closer to peek in the dirty window, when that black Crow flew by me screaming--- as if a warning of what was to come. I couldn't see much though. The window had years of crap on it. Sara was still standing at the car with her arms cross looking down at the dirt.

I watched her for a second when she looked up at me and said, "Hey sis, what's up? You're acting like you are ten again, crazy girl. I don't know if this was such a good idea."

"Just doing some flash backing, what do you mean sis? Hurry down here, I can almost smell the wood burning in the fireplace and the coffee my dad used to brew on it, can't you?" Thing was, I really could smell freshly burnt wood, odd I know... "Hey, I should have grabbed my old bear for this trip, remember him?" I shot back.

"OMG, you still have that ratty old thing? And yes, I remember it too," laughed Sara. She laughed, that was good.

"Hey Sara, let's go in and check out my old cabin, do you remember the sleepovers we had here?"

She gave me a long silent stare. Sara replied with reluctance in her eyes, and her arms crossed again. Now almost in a frightened state, like she was afraid to move. I guess I should have stopped to ask what was wrong, but I was too excited, lost in the past to stop and ask.

I headed to the door on the dockside of the cabin to see if it was open. I grabbed the handle, and turned it back and forth with no luck.

As I stood there working out a plan, which was to climb in the kitchen window if I had to, I heard a click, then the sound of a another click and the door suddenly started to creep open with Sara standing there not exactly smiling, but there she was in my cabin. What was up with her all of a sudden? All this sadness...

"Well now, how did you get in, dear sister?"

In a dull tone, she replied, "I used my key. I come here quite often to play, will you play with me!" A string of words, my sister's words---I will adopt soon, for my own meaning of the word *play*... The meaning will be quite different for me though.

Sara stepped back to let me in, she seemed very stiff, reserved almost. She had a dimness and distance in her eyes; she turned and walked over to the space between the kitchen and living room. I watched as her eyes started to mist with tears as she stood and looked at the kitchen table, the kitchen table of all things. I couldn't put my finger on it at that moment, still giddy about being home. I thought she might just be remembering our times here. Once again, I let it go.

I stepped in, further focusing on the room; I could see dirt and dust had overwhelmed the wood floors and furniture, what was left anyway. I walked over to the kitchen window that looked out onto our little dock at the Bayou, and lost myself in the past for just a minute---images of kids and families having summer fun all around me. Dad sitting outside on the dock reading one of his beloved sci-fi paperback books, while all the kids played on the little playground. Good times in all. What I didn't know was the truth, our truth apparently...

Then Sara startled me by saying something, which knocked me back from the past, but I didn't respond. I just stepped up to the ladder, the ladder I had climbed so many times as a little girl. The ladder looked clean; I mean really clean - no dust or dirt, almost polished. I ran my hands over the rungs as I took it all in, my fingers hit small bits of what seemed to be wax, little splashes up and down the ladder, giving the ladder a shiny multi colored glow, I noticed the kitchen table was the same...

The shiny wax dots were out of place in this dirt filled cabin---that was for sure. I looked back at Sara, and she still had a look of absence in her eyes, as if she was somewhere else. Her arms were by her sides with both fists clinched tight. She was almost shaking as she looked at the kitchen table. I thought she was getting mad at me, but again I was lost in my own world... I took another step up while gripping one of the leather straps at the top of the ladder and pulled myself up. Straps, I didn't remember them being there. That was just weird. My mind was racing to take in as much as I could, as fast as I could. It seemed to shut everything else out and flooded me with my childhood.

Sara was standing behind me at the base of the ladder, looking up at me with those big brown eyes, and she was tugging on my dress. In a whisper, she said "Hey sis, let's get out of here please. Let's see what else we can find, please, for me."

I didn't pay her any attention again, as I was caught up in my own selfish world at the moment. I should have listened, but I just stepped up on the ladder making my way to the loft. Half way up my head hit the ceiling and I had to swing a leg over, it wasn't this small back then, but I've grown a little since those days, for sure.

I had to roll myself onto the loft floor, putting me just where my sleeping bag used to lie. As I flopped down on the wooden planks, a cloud of dirt and dust filled the air making me sneeze. As I lay there looking out the small, really small, porthole window to the Bayou, I was a little girl again---that window was as big as the moon some nights. Of course, that was from the eyes of a little girl. I think I was lost again in the past because I didn't notice or hear Sara hovering over me, as she stood on the ladder looking down at me.

"Hello Sis, what are you doing up here---it's dirty, come back down---we need to go, this is getting creepy," she insisted. At least she didn't seem mad at me...

I looked up at her and asked, "Hey, Sara, do you remember the sleepovers we used to have up here?"

"Yeah, I do Raven, more than you will ever know, those sleepovers were the safest times of my childhood, the safest, the very safest." She kept repeating 'safest', with a hypnotic tone and look in her eyes, as she gazed out the porthole window, her face transfixed with joy and pain together. 'OMG, I need some Mary, up in this cabin---I'll buy the Italian biscuits for her, I thought to myself.'

I thought that statement was a little out of place for her. Of course what did I know about her---a mask of reserve seemed to cover her face now, but before I could ask her where she was in her head, Sara grabbed my arm and pulled me to the edge of the loft, chanting "Will you play with me, will you play with me?" those words again, that would haunt me later and forever...

We both slid down the ladder, and began to make our way out the front door. When I turned for one last look at the cabin, as we slowly closed the door behind us, Sara said, "Sorry, I needed to get out of there."

Sara held my hand tight as we walked past the playground and picnic area. We were on our way to the beach beyond those tall waving cypress and willow trees. I remember climbing them as kids and we had this awesome rope swing down by the water like the one on our dock---it was the best of the best on those hot sticky summer days, and it gets really hot and sticky here in the Bayou.

Sara pulled away, and put her toes in the water, the green yucky sluggish water, then all of a sudden, she went ankle deep in the yuck of green Bayou water.

"Gross girl, what are you doing?" I asked.

"Doing a little of my own flash backing of my own, Raven. Sis, there are things, so many things from my past, my innocence, that you have no idea of: things I can't tell anyone, things I've had to keep inside, things no one should ever tell. These things have shaped the person I have become," Sara said as she looked out into the green Bayou while flicking the green yuck back and forth with her foot.

"Sara, what things, talk to me---we have found each other after all this time, we are family now, you have someone to listen, not judge you, but to listen and help in whatever way you need---Sara, I want to be there for you. Maybe I can't erase the past, but we can work through it together now."

Sara just stood silent with her arms crossed and firsts balled tight, looking out into the Bayou. I was reluctant to walk over, but I must have been already walking while my mind was thinking this out, because I was hugging Sara from behind, resting my chin on her shoulder before I knew it.

I could feel her trembling as she reached up and took hold of my arms, I've never had to do anything like this, with anybody---I don't know if I have what it takes---where is Mary when I need her, right...? I know being alone most of my life didn't help me with trying to help Sara, but this felt right, and I have family now. I must be strong for Sara.

I got in front of Sara and cupped her face with my hands, telling her how important she was in my life right now and helping her through whatever was going on was my only focus now.

Sara shook her head, breaking my hands free from her face as she began ranting, "Raven, you're so innocent, this isn't what you think. I'm not on drugs or an alcoholic or have a gambling problem. This goes deeper than that; much, deeper and darker.

It's, well---something, something---um, something---well, maybe we can---maybe---well, ok, shit-shit-shit! Raven, let's go out to dinner next Sunday, we can talk after you feed me and get me wined up," she replied.

"Sara, that is a week away, this is important, I don't want to wait, please talk to me, let's go to the car and sit down and talk, ok?"

"Yes, Raven, I know it's next week, but I have work stuff and things to get fixed first. We can meet on Sunday for Sara's confession dinner, my confession, my coming out party---finally, it will be good, I think I'm almost ready to tell someone my life, my secrets. Hell, you could probably write a damn book and make a million or do a movie for Lifetime with it, something, and it's really that good."

Sara turned and darted up the path back to the cabins, leaving me standing ankle deep in slush feeling I wasn't any help. I could see she was hurting with something. I realized at that moment, I didn't know anything about how she grew up, her parents, school, friends, or influences she had had in her life. This empty life shit is getting me angry.

I kicked the green sludge spinning me around facing the Bayou again. I was angry, really angry, at my dad or whoever he was, for not telling me I had a sister from another marriage or whatever. I guess that's what it was; again, we don't know what or how any of this happened.

I noticed a flickering light from the old boathouse on the north end of the Bayou, where most of the fishing and boat rentals happened. And that small store full of candy, soda and ice cream, a kid's dream. I could almost see the famous ping pong table that rested on the upper deck. We sure lost a lot of balls over the summers here.

I could see a man and his dog stepping out of the boathouse and walking along the edge of the water, heading towards the cabins. I ran up the path to find Sara, I found her alright. She was standing in an old swing on the playground with her head hanging down and her wrists were wrapped in the chains above her head while she slowly glided back and forth, she couldn't have seen the man coming, she was facing the other direction.

I stood there for a second watching her with her wrists bound in the chains, swinging back and forth, in her own world, what world? Those chains had to hurt, I thought, just odd.

"Sara, there is someone coming, look."

She jumped out of the swing and ran up behind me, looking over my shoulder at the figure in the distance; she was shaking and said we must get out of here.

I began to step forward to go and greet the man, when Sara grabbed my waist to stop me, and said, "Raven, this isn't a good idea; we don't know him or what he might do? Let's just go."

As the man got closer, I could see that he had a limp on the left side, but he had this gentle old look overall. His dog ran up and sat in front of us, tail wagging and smacking his chops ready to play. I could tell the ole boy had some age on him, but he seemed spirited. His master now standing right in front of us, I could see his old weathered face and beautiful crystal blue eye, he only had one eye, the other was just a dead hole nothing there but a piece of skin, sunk in a little. He lit up with a smile as if he knew us.

"Nice to see you girls again, all grown up, I see. The place is a little old and shabby but enjoy your visit and remember to stay out of my tomatoes, they are world class this year," as the man wandered off towards the beach.

Sara looked at me with her face in a scrunch and said, "Ok, how crazy was that, tomatoes, nice to see us again?"

I spun around looking at the old man and his dog as they walked down the Bayou edge toward the beach. I grabbed Sara's arm and whispered in her ear, "Was it crazy---was it crazy, Sara? Follow me."

I let her go and started down the path to catch up to the old man, while Sara hesitated. She wasn't too sure this was a good idea, but followed me anyway, chirping, "What are you doing, Raven, we don't know this man."

I looked over my shoulder and said, "Follow me, follow me, Sara, back to the past, our past, Sara. I remember the tomatoes... And his name is Henry, I'm sure of it."

"All those summers watching out that little round porthole in my loft, I remembered a man with his dog in a boat out on the lake fishing every night, just after dinner. Then the next morning there would be fresh fish and home-grown tomatoes on our dock. I think this could be that man--- Henry was his name. He might remember something, it was worth a chance. It's all we have right now. "Sara, he could be that old man, he could have answers."

"What old man?" yelled Sara.

Chapter 4

The Awakening Begins

'You gain strength, courage, and confidence by every experience in which you really stop to look fear in the face. You are able to say to yourself, "I lived through this horror. I can take the next thing that comes along.'

Eleanor Roosevelt

The honk of an ambulance horn and flash of blue lights hit my closed eyes as we rolled up the dirt path. We were here: here where my life started all those years ago and Sara's life has ended so painfully. I still haven't told Jack it was us, exploring up here the other day. I'm sure he will find out, sooner than later if he is as good as I believe he is, a very intense man. I just don't know if I can or should trust them. I know they are the police, but for some reason I just can't.

In the distance I noticed two men wading in the yuck the Bayou had become after all these years. They had those black rubber diving suits on with masks and air tanks. One of them had a stick thing he was using to pluck in and out of the water, while the other guy had a camera snapping away.

I turned in my seat to look back at the dirt road leading in, all I could see were police cars, vans, SUVs and a fire truck, all with lights flashing, all lining the dirt road on both sides. Down at the entrance of the path that led to the picnic area sat an ambulance with its back doors open. I could see two men or maybe a woman gathering stuff through the windshield of the ambulance. They were loading it on a stretcher. Of course, that sent my mind wild with flashes of Sara. I could hear dogs barking behind me and see people passing the car as I sat there.

Radios were squawking with words you couldn't understand, but somehow the police did. Lights were flashing all over the place. At that moment I threw my hands over my ears to stop the noise, to just shut it out. I wanted to run, run and hide, maybe in my old cabin. Hide up in my little loft with my bear Henry and sleeping bag, the way I remembered, while I stared out my little porthole window at the moon and caught my peace, the peace of my loft. Yes, my peace was now gone.

A POP sounded---the car door came open, sending a rush of cool Bayou air flooding in. It slapped me sober with the reality of today's events. I stood just outside the car looking at the mist drifting through the trees and settling on the Bayou. The Bayou always smelled so fresh in the mornings, it was always very peaceful, but not today. In less than five minutes my world was going to be flipped upside down.

Why was I here? This seemed wrong---nothing like anything you see in the movies or on TV, the relatives never went to the crime scene---not that we live our lives according to TV, right...? Why had they brought me here? What were they up to? Do they think I did it---my own sister? I may be going crazy, but I'm not there yet!

Jack reached and took my hand again to start us down the dirt path to the crime scene behind my cabin, of all places, really... All I could see was that yellow crime scene tape everywhere, with little flashes of light flickering from all directions. Jack grabbed my arm as the man with the stretcher flew by us, followed by the female EMT carrying a large red bag over her shoulder both headed to the dock of the cabin. She gave me a glance as they passed.

Jack burst out with, "Don't move anything until we have had a chance to see it first, please."

I saw the EMT's cut Jack a look.

"Like, this is my first murder scene, dude?" The EMT shouted.

"Sorry guys, this is Raven, THE VICTIM'S SISTER! Raven may help shed some light on what happened out here. We haven't been down there yet, that is all I meant, guys," Jack said with clenched teeth.

They paused before the male EMT said, "No worries man, we will give you some time." They fully understood what Jack was up to, and I was beginning to get a clue as well. They went back up to the ambulance to wait. I had to look up now, it was time and I had to try not to think about what these guys were leading me to. The wind picked up at that moment, like Sara was helping me stay on my feet.

Trust me I was ready to fall over and vomit. It was as if I were drunk without drinking any wine. I was getting the dizzies, and my knees did that snap thing---when they are about to give out. Jack held me tight under my arm to prevent me from falling. We had reached the yellow crime scene tape that circled the cabin and back dock, but then we stopped. I don't think anyone was ready for this.

Detective Oliver Dupeux was just ahead of us talking to a police guy closer to the spot where Sara was. Agent Jack Bode' still had my arm as another officer walked over to us. Jack asked the officer to stay with me while they ran down to the water and checked the scene before I got down there. They were telling him this while they both pulled out blue rubber gloves out of their back pockets and snapped them open like this was just a regular day at the office---not that they were going to look at my dead Sister as I stood right in front of them.

"Cold, very cold, guys, really!" I blurted out, with a look on my face that could stop traffic and it did actually---everyone froze. Then they backed away from me slowly as they ran off to play or whatever it is they do before they totally destroy someone's life.

I got a chill and crossed my arms as I stood there waiting, I could feel my fingernails digging into my upper arms, with thoughts of not knowing, I had to shut my eyes and turned around to face the playground in the distance. All I could picture was Sara in the swing with her wrists wrapped in the chains, that painful sight. What was she trying so desperately to tell me?

Time was standing still once again, as I began to drift back to the other day when Sara and I were here at the Bayou, when she grabbed my arm and asked, "What the hell was I thinking?"

I looked in her eyes, her big brown eyes, and said, "Mom and Dad, Sara, he has the answers. Sara, the old man is Henry, from our summers here---he must know something?" Sara let go, as if she had been hit in the head with a hammer at that moment. It would turn out, that Henry did know everything---more than everything, as I would discover later, and Sara knew that too, but she stood there for a while. I ran a few steps ahead to catch the old man. I was reaching out for his shoulder---when Jack and Oliver suddenly popped out from around the corner of the cabin startling me back from my back flashing, they could see that something, visibly shook me.

I must have had that ghost face on, as Oliver wasted no time in asking me what I was reaching for, then with the questions, then another, he was like a machine gun---rapid firing in my face.

"Did you remember something, Raven?"

I reached out for Jack's shoulder to steady myself; he grabbed me as they took quick glances at each other. They could tell I was ready to pass out.

"Raven, are you ok? You seem a little out of it?" asked Jack.

My hand touched Jack's chest as I fell against him. I could feel his heart beating like a drum through his shirt. I began to gently slide down him, on my way to the ground. Jack was telling Oliver something. I tried to listen to what Jack was saying, but things were just garbled and in slow motion like a dream again, or a heavy wined up night. I knew I knew I was fading out; I wasn't coming back from this flashback, not at all...

"Ma'am, what did you just see?" Oliver shouted.

They both called to me, my mouth went dry, and I could actually feel my eyes roll back in my head, and then everything went silent. At that point, my left leg just gave out. I fell to one knee as my face slid down Jack's body. I must have grabbed hold of his belt buckle while falling face first into the black muck, how embarrassing. Jack swooped in grabbing me under my arms while flipping me over at the same time right before my face hit the black muck.

I must have been out for a while, and then suddenly I felt my head snap back as if I had been hit from behind---an awful taste filled my mouth and the smell of horseradish shot up my nose consuming me. My eyes popped open to Jack's face, a beautiful intense face with bright blue eyes. How nice, considering he was waving something under my nose that smelled awful---he was talking to me, but I couldn't hear anything he was saying or anything around me for that matter---what an eerie feeling that was!

I watched his lips; he was saying my name---Raven, Raven, over and over again. I felt myself start to float up to meet his lips with mine when Oliver snapped his fingers in my left ear and every sound from the Bayou came flooding in with a POP, startling me back into reality once again.

I'm beginning to see that the dream-time or flash backing, I have been doing the past couple of weeks now, are more my thing. At least, while there in dream-time I'm safe and getting answers. I'm wishing now, I could just stay there in dream-time moments for a while. It might seem a little safer than the Bayou at this point. Here in reality, all I'm getting is pain, pain, and more pain---that's the real world, right...? This must be how crazy feels? I just have to wonder...

They both lifted me up and walked me to the back of the ambulance where they sat me on the back edge. The female EMT wrapped a blanket around me then handed me a cup of hot peppermint tea, telling me it would help clear my head for what was just ahead.

That just seemed odd, who has peppermint tea handy? I thought, the day just gets wierder as the minutes tick on. What she didn't tell me was that the tea was really for the smell, the decomposition of the body. My sister's body, which was left to rot, like trash by that ass hole. Jack asked if I was doing better, I nodded yes, but really didn't want to say yes. We all knew I wasn't really ok, was this the plan? To see if I would break down, well, they got their answer.

"Raven, do you think we can take you down to the cabin, so you can identify the body and then we'll get you home to rest? We don't want to lose the light of the day. It's getting late and the Bayou gets dark quickly."

"Hello, ma'am, do you understand"? Oliver said in a sharp tone.

I watched as every word fell from his mouth, and I could feel his breath push against my face. I was still feeling a little dizzy, my mouth was still dry, so nothing was able to come out, but my brain was running a thousand miles a minute. All I could think was why would they want me to actually see the crime scene, unless they thought maybe I did it?

"Shit, really?"---what were they keeping from me.

His grip on my arm just got tighter, as he began walking me down the path to my old cabin again. We stopped at the rear corner of the cabin, that's when I looked up and saw her---Sara, my little sister---my only family, hanging there, in the tree that once held a rope swing from our summers. Now that rope was wrapped around her body holding her up there in the tree, hanging over the Bayou.

My body went instantly stiff, cold and shaking violently. I was about to lose my cookies, but the urge just left me, but a sharp stabbing pain ran through my head. The pain was very intense, and it landed behind my right eye. It was as if flashbulbs were going off all around me. I couldn't stop looking at her open eyes. Those eyes seemed to hold me together or what looked like me being all together, but I wasn't. I could feel my heart beating so fast it made me feel faint and breathless.

Sara---Sara was lying face up on what looked like a wood plank with that thick rope around her and the plank, it was fashioned into a large noose, she was dressed in all black, jacket with no shirt, exposing her black lace bra, her arms dangling to each side with her legs hanging off the end of the plank almost touching the water. She still had her black heels on. How does something like this happen? I could see what looked like a perfect spiral of blood twisting around her right sleeve, like an artist's tattoo.

The blood formed a perfect pool floating on top of the thick green muck of the Bayou. Camera flashes were popping all around as we stood looking at her beautiful face. Her face was turned to look down at whoever would find her. Those big brown eyes still open, but very empty now, she was gone. I couldn't stop looking at them; they were very cold and lifeless for someone once so full of life. Sara hung there breathless like a painting. A vision that will never leave me now... This will never stop haunting me!

I stood there seeing something no one should ever have to see---why did they do this to me---why? I could understand them taking me to the hospital to identify her but why did they bring me here to see this---I remember looking at Sara, and quietly asking her what am I supposed to do now? I don't know if I actually said that out-loud or if it was in my head. Here comes the crazy...

Then, clear as day, Sara spoke down to me... "Vengeance, Raven, Vengeance." It was as if Sara transferred her pain down to me at that moment.

Vengeance--- echoed though my head, over and over again like a metal pin ball zipping through, landing right behind my right eye causing those bright flashes and getting worse by the second. The pain was so bad by this point, I put my hands over my eye and shouted, "What, Sara, what am I to do?"

My heart stopped, my knees felt weak, my eyes rolled back in my head, as I flopped backwards to the ground in a seizure, with the burning images of Sara looking at me, flashing in my head. Minutes passed as I lay on the ground beneath the tree, hidden between its roots jerking in all directions as if possessed by demons and no one around noticing what was happening.

The EMT that was on his way down to the dock with the stretcher for Sara, saw my foot shaking between the roots and began yelling; "Guys, she's down---she's down!" His voice echoed through the Bayou.

Chapter 5

Graduation

'We must let go of the life we have planned, so as to accept the one that is waiting for us.'

Joseph Campbell

LSU, Tiger Stadium. Graduation day 2012. Standing there in the middle of the field, by myself of course---while all around me were parents, moms and dads laughing and hugging their children. They seemed proud and relieved all at once.

I stood there for hours just watching, when a hand touched my shoulder sending chills down my back. I turned to see my favorite teacher and sometimes step-in dad, Professor Taylor, standing there with his wife, Jan. Professor Taylor reached out his arms and hugged me like a daughter, and then Jan stepped in and held us both. I could feel Jan shaking as she cried. Wow, I didn't know what to think of that.... But it made me smile anyway.

For a moment, I felt as if I was part of a family, but that didn't last long. Missy, a friend of sorts broke the circle of hugs, yelling, "We've got to get our stuff out of the room---come on, I need to turn in the key." Missy rushed off in a huff as she usually does. That's a girl I won't miss.

Professor Taylor told me how proud they were of me for all the hard work I had put in to get here. As I wiped a tear from my eye, yes, only one tear, and that was good for me, understand. I haven't cried since childhood I believe, truly cried. They asked me to come to the lake house for the weekend, to enjoy this time with them. I was still a little frozen in the moment but said yes. I let them know I was almost done packing and would head out to the lake house once I loaded my stuff.

Professor Taylor replied; "Dinner at seven!"

I could really use a little lake time right now, to organize my head, to focus on my next move to my great love, New Orleans. I am to start my new job this next Wednesday, life begins, right...?

Well, some other students of his just grabbed professor Taylor and Jan for pictures, so I made my way to my apartment on the west side of the campus for the last time. It was a walk of grace, so to speak.

I had finished my college career with a 4.0, a handful of design honors, a junior design winner for the coastal project in New Orleans, and let me tell you, I was on top of my game---the best Architect in my class, just unstoppable, my professor would say.

Right now---today is the moment we students work towards, FREEDOM and a new life---once I step off these grounds it will be my world to make out there, alone. One of my professors would often tell me that alone is what has made me strong. I loved our talks. I'm making this sound so sad, but it's a new chapter and I'm really excited. Right, I mean life?

You would think so, but it seems like I'm taking the right steps, but with something missing---sounds crazy to me, it's just a feeling I have, a stirring of sorts. Car packed, this is my life in four suitcases. Standing in front of the only thing I actually own, my car, a bright red Mini Cooper convertible. Ziggy is his name---he's been good to me over these 4 years.

Ziggy is a funny story. Just as I was about to leave for LSU, a check came in the mail for $32,000 dollars. The check was written to me with a beautiful hand-written note which read, 'Make your future, don't let anything or anybody get in the way--make it your own.' I had no idea who sent me $32,000 dollars. I had no relatives; no life insurance money from mom or dad, nothing, yet a check for $32,000 pops up out of nowhere. Now that I think of it, I never had to pay a dime for school either - I mean college. I was told at admissions that all is covered and all I had to do was learn and graduate. The mystery soup thickens, right?

Well, I headed out to the professor's house, the long drive down highway 10 with Ziggy's top down, music playing, wind blowing my hair all over, cuz I couldn't find a hair tie. I must say it gave me a lot of space to day-dream about the next chapter of my adventure.

I reached the driveway about 6pm. As I turned in and slowed to take in the view, I thought, "My God, I love this place!" Over the last four years, there have been many weekends spent here drawing and relaxing. Many of those weekends I would set myself adrift in Professor T's wooden boat and just drift and cloud watch for hours. My evening favorite was sitting on the dock in the big wooden chairs, reading and thinking the weekends away.

I noticed Jan was sitting on the steps out front reading her new book of the month, waiting for me. Through my years here at LSU, Jan has helped me along the way too, not having or knowing my Mom in the later years, Jan filled in some of the pieces, she really seemed to care.

Professor T tried his best to instill the "fatherly" stuff; you know - boys, dating, tattoos---a big one, and no body piercing, a super big one. Then, he would talk about money, music, and education. Poor guy, he just didn't understand girls---most fathers don't, really. At least he gave the harder stuff a try. He fumbled a lot, but thank God, he tried and that has gone a long way. It's so true about fathers and most men in general, they just melt under a daughter's spell---they become like play dough in our hands.... All hail the power of a daughter!

I jumped out to give her a hug, almost forgetting to put my car in park. I pushed myself into her arms and asked her what she was reading, as I held her tight.

"This is my book of the month, of course. I'm really into this reading phase at the moment. This one is from James Patterson 'Guilty Wives.' I started it last week."

I shot back with, "Guilty Wives, something you want to share."

She smiled a half smile while reaching for another hug. Jan pulled me in and whispered in my ear - "You're going to be alright girl, I know so, you are ready for what life throws at you, make it your own." I didn't move, frozen from that statement---I just stayed in her arms, as she trembled and sniffed. I knew I wanted this feeling to last as long as possible. I had missed this for a big part of my life. It always felt special with Jan, I don't know why, but it did.

Jan let me go and took my hand as we walked into the house. She told me to head out to the dock and relax for a while. Professor T would bring in my stuff from the car. I saw the lake through the open door, it was calling me. My feet just kept walking until I reached the end of the dock. I think I walked right past Professor T in the kitchen as if I were in a trance. I walked straight to the edge with my toes hanging over the last plank of the dock. My God, how I missed this, I could feel the pressures just fall off me. I stood there looking out over the quiet waters of the lake with all the houses that dotted the shore line. I could see some had their lights on through the trees, and it was so pretty. As it began to get darker the lightning bugs started to arrive. Sending me right back to the Bayou nights and the fun times I had there---innocent times.

I was still hugging that last dock pole as I flashed back in time, not noticing Jan behind me with a tray of drinks. By the way, she makes the best all-around drink, we named it 'Jan's Summertime Cucumber Gin Lake Smash', and well, Lake Smash to be honest---the real name was too long for us college kids. You would be sober by the time you said the whole name. Now we drank a lot of Smash over the past four years here at the lake. Professor T always said, "There are no age limits on the lake property, ha, ha."

That was a special rule - only here, though. I turned to see Jan place the tray on the table at dock chairs and sit down.

"Honey, come sit with me and talk a while," she said in her slow, southern French Louisiana tone---after all, Jan is a straight up Cajun, packing a PHD of course. Her tone, it is very soft and very hypnotic. I always wondered why they had no kids. I never asked them. Jan would have made a great mom - she is one person that could get me to talk about things that I normally would be guarded about.

Now that I think about it, her Lake Smash may have been her secret all along. That's the WHY my mouth was so out of control with her, right? No, not really, she is just easy to talk to---that's all, like a mom. I really thought of her that way sometimes, I really did...

Jan looked over at me and said, "Honey, you have that look again---the same one you had the first time you found your way out here to the lake. Raven, I'm also very thankful you found your way to us all those years ago, baby girl."

I looked at her for a long time without a word, sometimes which says a lot, and then came the tears, real tears. I hadn't let go like that since the funeral of my parents. My eyes just rained tears. I really don't act like this, what is up with me? I have built myself up on a tough no nonsense life, now I'm crying.

Jan reached over and took my hand and said, "You're out on your own now. It has to be hard not really having anyone to be your back up. Raven, what I mean is we are here for you, and honey, I hope you know that, baby girl... You're the closest thing to a daughter I will ever have, and, well sweetie---we do love you, but... Please believe we are here for you."

Jan stood with her arms out, waiting for a hug. I jumped into her arms, holding her tight, thinking that she just left something out of her talk a second ago, what was it and why? *Jan has more to* tell, and for some reason she is holding something back. My entire short life began to play in my head, the brief years with my parents---really not a lot there, other than the times at the Bayou and then fast forwarding into college. From that point it was the lake house, the Taylor's. Then I had nothing. There is nothing in between, but lost years, and fast years. What does all this mean?

Up on the deck, Professor T started ringing that huge brass bell, the dinner bell. Jan broke our hug and turned to him and yelled, "Really, you big goof - it's just us, not the usual crew..." Her hands on her hips as she shook her head. I just stood behind her for one last smile, repeating in my head, "Here's to all the fun memories this place has meant to me."

I really had no idea if I would ever be back here, so I wanted to take in every moment, the more moments I could get the better. It was as if something inside was preparing me for something, that feeling I keep having? That stirring or stomach acid, whichever, whatever... It was something different than the normal me I know... I guess I wrote it off as my new life, which started the second I drove off campus and hit highway 10, right? I think, this is the beginning of the awakening, where life turns itself on, the stirring from within...

"Guess we better get up there before he goes bell crazy." Jan said.

Jan darted up the dock toward the house, and I followed slowly behind her. I stopped next to the bell to watch Jan and Professor T set the table together, laughing and picking at each other---that's real, I thought. A couple, a family and she asked me to be part of it, basically.

Could I do that? I have only had that for a brief moment in time. I have really been alone the majority of my 21 years of life. Life is a strange thing. How does a family begin? What makes the connection? Why do people find certain people?

I felt so empty inside sometimes, well most times---and the empty, blank, and nothing feeling, always there. I know I am one of those people that could switch people off---or on, whichever suited me at that time---for the most part in my life the switch has been off, for most people in my life---especially if I had no use for them. I just flip that switch---click, they are no more. That sounds cold, to do to someone. Well, I guess I'm cold to stupid people, and as we all know most people have a lot of stupid! Would Mary call this a kind of disorder or is this how crazy really works?

Jan yelled down to me, "Honey, come in and eat," as she stood at the French doors, unaware I was standing just outside at the bell, watching them play together. At that moment I was somewhere else in my head, one of my foggy thinking moments came rolling in from far away.

I've been doing that more and more lately. Anyway, I smiled as I stepped in and sat in the same chair I had always sat in for the four years of coming to the lake---what does that say? We all began passing food and laughing, talking about summers here and school breaks we spent at the lake, the whole crew of course. The Lake House and Taylor's were our go-to place. It actually provided a safe place for us to come and enjoy a quiet weekend.

Professor T asked me what my next adventure was. I looked his way with a smile and said, "Well, work starts next week---house hunting needs to happen soon, I guess." He began talking about house stuff, I think. I wasn't getting any of what he was saying, my head was somewhere else again, still lost in the fog and that stirring thing...

Jan saw I wasn't in the conversation, and jumped in with, "HEY, would like you like us to come to New Orleans and help you look, if you're ok with that?" I shot back with a "Wow, you guys would do that with me?"

"Of course, we would love to be part of that with you, Raven. We think of you as part of the family and I love me some Orleans food, baby...." We all just laughed at Professor T as he patted his stomach, he is a true foodie. I started clearing the table with Jan, the whole time running on about how fun it would be to help pick out the furniture and curtains and, and, and...

She was really getting into the mom thing I guess, which I'm not used to and don't really know how to navigate that, so I just let her run on for a while. I know she means well and all, but... I was starting to feel pressure, so I made my escape to the dock to relax and think. Sitting out there in one of the big wooden chairs with a glass of Lake Smash, has always felt good and helped me to de-stress and focus. In my everyday life I never stopped long enough to ask questions of myself, I just kept moving forward, pushing to be the best at whatever I was doing, always chasing, never stopping to reflect. Chasing was something I was very good at, what was I really chasing though…?

I'm a girl who doesn't know her past, has no idea of any relatives, and knows nothing about her parent's past. I have a blank past, no paper trail or pictures, who was I really - how did I get past the college admissions? Who gave me $32,000 dollars? High school would have been easy, but college boards... and yet here I sit, a graduate.

I tipped the smash to the sky to take the last drop, "Gone---more I say, more---I stood up to sneak in the kitchen and pour another when I noticed a tray with a carafe of lake smash and fruit with a note that read "thought you may need some more thinking power baby girl, Jan." She is just so cool.

"Cheers to you, Jan," as I poured another and sat ready for the nightly fog to roll back in---I mean lake fog, not my head fog, but you never know, right... One glass led to two and then another...

I must have fallen asleep in the chair on the dock, when I flashed on Professor T's face. He was lifting me in his arms, as he walked up the dock towards the house, I bounced gently in his arms, as crickets and frogs sang all around. I had a vision of the Bayou and the cabins, like a Deja vu moment followed with other flashes but I couldn't make those out - damned Lake Smash.

He took me upstairs, softly opened the bedroom door with his foot and carefully laid me in bed, putting the throw blanket from the foot of the bed over me. Professor T stood for a moment looking down at me with a smile and a concerned look, all mashed together at same time. I watched him leave the room and shut the door. That was a nice feeling, a family feeling, now it's time to dream, dream, dream... what were those flashes?

Morning hit my face as I sat up in bed to get some clarity. I needed to try and remember those visions of the Bayou. It was that motion, the light bouncing motion as he walked, the soft bounce, the sway of my arm and legs that triggered the flash.

For some reason this is important, but nothing is coming, a blank like always. That's my life, a blank---I can't seem to get the pieces to come together. I mean life, my life. I have no fucking idea of what the past is trying to tell me. I threw on some sweats and headed to the coffee pot downstairs. Coffee, coffee, I needed coffee...

Professor T was sitting at the kitchen table watching a canoe go by down on the lake, while sipping his coffee. I said good morning in a grumpy tone. He twisted his head my way and replied, "Are you ok, sweetie?"

"Yes, a bad night, a lot of lake smash and dreams---dreams I can't seem to put together."

I stepped out the door and headed to the lake, not wanting to get involved in a conversation at the moment. As I rushed down the dirt path, a path I had walked down for many years, mind you, I saw the willow tree root, the same root I have stepped over every time while visiting Professor T, but this time my toe slipped under the root and down I flew, coffee flying in the air and I saw the dirt rushing up at me.

'SMACK', face first in the dirt. Stars circled my head as I tried to push myself up, but my arms gave out and out I went...

Chapter 6

THE STIRRING AWAKENS

'There are two great days in a person's life - the day we are born and the day we discover why!'

William Barclays

The words of the EMT echoed across the Bayou, "She's down"...

Jack turned to see my body bouncing between the tree roots. He ran to me and leaped to the ground, sliding his body underneath me, with my face inches from smacking the black sticky muck and tree roots. Jack pulled me into his arms. The EMT grabbed Jack's shoulder yelling down to him, "Jack, turn her on her side, she is seizing---watch her for any vomiting, and keep her mouth clear." The EMT looked back at us again, and told Jack to hold my head so I don't hit it on anything, but let my body flex and flop.

Jack looked down painfully, as he held my shaking head in his hands. The EMT leaped back and forth over us and landed on the opposite side of my body. He checked my pulse, while stabilizing my legs a bit almost at the same time. Jack leaned forward to check my mouth for vomit, they say timing is everything, right---I blew a load right in front of poor Jack, making him fell back into the muck, while watching my body shake, wrench and twist like I was having a mind-blowing orgasm between the tree roots and the black sticky dirt of the Bayou. Mind-blowing is exactly what was happening to me. Flashes of Sara, one after another, she was hanging from the tree. Sara was looking down at me one second, with a tear falling from her eye, then the two of us on my living room floor laughing and sipping wine the next.

Then back to the misty Bayou with red and blue lights flickering through the trees. Then flashes of when we were little girls playing right here--- little Sara swinging back and forth with no worries. Then the figure of a man walking with me in his arms lightly bouncing while crickets and frogs sang in the night, then finally shadowy figures of men and women in all kinds of masquerade masks, black capes some wearing hoods. They were all holding objects in their hands, but I couldn't see clearly. They seemed to be standing in a circle around a single person, up on something. What was I watching?

Twenty minutes had passed before I opened my eyes; I was still lying at the base of the tree. I could feel someone holding me. It was Jack, of course. Oliver was standing next to him showing him some pictures. I just laid there looking up at my sister---they hadn't moved her yet.

I was thinking, who could have done this? What kind of person does this to someone else? What was she into to make someone do this? My sister Sara was gone, all that was left, were memories. I focused on the rope, the hang-man's knot holding my sister in the air, swinging in the breeze, back and forth over the water we once played in.

I began to sit up slowly with the help of Jack; he eased me into a sitting position and held me there for a second to make sure I could sit up on my own. Oliver began questioning me right away, but Jack held his hand up to stop him, saying, "Give her a second to come back. She has to be groggy from the seizure, go get the EMT and let's make sure."

Jack put his hand on my shoulder and began asking slowly, with a soft tone, "Raven, are you ok? We were a little worried about you. I have never seen anything like that," he said.

I brushed my hair back and said, "I think I'm ok. What happened?"

Jack reached out and touched my face and held my chin gently, telling me I had just had a seizure and was out for about twenty minutes. As he spoke, his eyes stayed fixed on mine as they burned into me. I could feel my heart give me a nervous jolt and my body began to tingle inside as he looked at me. His grip tightened on my left arm, what the hell was happening to me? My sister was murdered and I'm sitting here tingling in a man's arms.

"Really, Raven," I told myself, "This is not what I need to be doing right now. Finding Sara's killer is what needs to happen. Life just turned left on a one-way street for me. A Street named, 'Vengeance' echoed in my head.

Jack stood up next to Oliver. While I sat there and looked up at Sara and back at Jack. He had that lost puppy look, but I didn't have time for that. My mind was busy drafting the blueprints for my new project. I found myself drifting further and further away from Jack and the other investigators, as I slowly eased my way up the path. My mind began piecing together strings of information from the last couple of weeks with Sara, while filtering childhood memories and weaving them into a solid direction to find out what happened and who did this to my sister. And is all this related to the dreams?

Amazingly, no one was paying me any attention at the moment, as I floated up the path. It felt like I was invisible. The EMT went up to get me a blanket, and Jack was busy with the crime scene guys. I was all alone. I stopped at the kitchen door of the cabin, put my hand on the knob, but didn't go in, not yet---I wasn't ready for that... From where I was standing, I could see Sara's front bumper peeking out from the corner of the cabin at the top of the hill, so I made my way up there, while looking back to see who was watching, to my surprise, no cop guy's in sight, not a soul, I'm invisible...

I reached for the door handle and "click," it popped open. The keys were sitting on the passenger seat. So, I sat down and grabbed the steering wheel with both hands thinking of Sara. Outside I could hear the creepy squeaking of the rusty chains from the playground as the swings blew in the breeze and the crunch of footsteps coming up the pebble path, that's a sound that has always stuck with me, that crunch sound.

I saw that it was Jack coming at me in the side mirror. Jack touched my shoulder and asked if I was doing ok. I nodded without saying anything, hoping he would move in closer, but no, he knelt beside the car instead---he's such a gentleman. Jack squeezed my shoulder and let me be. He headed back down the trail. Wow, ok then, I slid the keys in my pocket and grabbed the CD hanging from the player and eased it in my bra for safe keeping. I noticed that there was nothing else in the car. No purse, where is her Black Coach purse she was never without?

As I sat back, I glanced in the rear-view mirror to see my cabin looking back at me, nothing else but my cabin. All I could think of *was 'Answers, 'there were answers in there*, that voice said again. I got out of the car and headed down the pebble path in front of playground right to the front door. I was still very surprised no law dudes were around; they were all either near the water or by the tree.

Once inside, I leaned back against the door and just looked around. The place looked the same as we left it, or so I thought at first glance. I went directly to the ladder, climbed to the top and stopped. I took a deep breath, grabbed hold of the ladder and turned my butt around resting it on one of the ladder rungs. I was facing the inside of the cabin now, which gave me a bird's eye view of everything. It was like looking down at a Clue game board while standing at a table---blueprints of sorts.

"Now it's your turn to talk to me, Mr. Cabin, talk." I said out loud.

I looked everything over from up there. I started at the front door it seemed like the logical place. I could see a path of scuffed dirt and crushed leaves and maybe footprints coming in from the front door. I followed them with my eyes right to the table in front of the kitchen. A chair had been slid back, a chair that was not there last weekend! An empty bowl was on the floor upside down, lying next to a candle, that wasn't there when we were last here either. Just under the table, almost hidden by leaves, I could see the glare of what may have been a belt buckle. It was a belt, a leather belt, I think?

I stepped down one rung at a time to take in the view from every level. I kind of feel like a Crime Scene Investigator, I might have made a good one.... I have a quick eye and do have a cool name that would be perfect for it, CSI Raven Rousseau and I'm cute, well, anyway? Now at the base of the ladder I did a 360 to see anything else, but nothing jumped out at me. I kneeled down under the edge of the table and grabbed the belt---it wasn't a belt at all, it was a leather flat whip with a brass end, I fell back against the kitchen cabinets with a gasp of disbelief.

Then to my left, I noticed a small piece of blue fabric peeking out from under the bottom lip of the cabinets. I crawled to it and could see that the wood floor boards were hiding something. I pulled at the blue fabric, and it popped the floorboards up leaving a dark opening. Holy shit, I sat there on the floor of the kitchen holding my sister's blue shirt.

I gave her that shirt. I started to cry as I held it against my face, I could smell her perfume. That vanilla sent. I just fell back against the cabinets for a second. I looked down again and I saw the strap to her purse peaking half out of the hole in the floor. I leaned over to pull it out and see what else was hiding in there. Outside cracks of thunder rang out just as I put my hand in the dark hole, freaky, then another crack and a flash of lightning. A storm was coming, a storm in more ways than one.

I laid everything out on the kitchen floor to look at its story, Sara's last chapter. What the hell was she doing here alone with someone, someone she never told me about?

"Little sister, what were you into that you couldn't tell me about?" I knew I should've pushed for more that day we were here. I took a breath while lightning flashes filled the windows. Ok---her blue ripped shirt, I started with the shirt and held it for a second. As I stepped back trying to put the puzzle together. Taking my time to walk through the cabin thinking, wishing I had given a little more attention to CSI Miami than I had. I was in front of the table just as a flash of lightning hit the windows, lighting up the cabin, which gave me the perfect picture of what was on the table---a dotted wax outline of a body, in different colored wax... there had to be several layers of it. What the hell...

I ran my hand along the tables edge picturing my sister laying naked, as my hand touched something sharp near the corner. It was a piece of fingernail sunken in wax and broken off. As another flash of lightning struck, I could see the gold speckled fingernail polish on it, Sara's polish! She was the one on the table for sure. This just gets worse by the minute, "Sara what the hell were you into?"

I could hear the police dogs and see the bouncing light from their flashlights getting near. I didn't move anything, I wanted Jack to see it all and see just what happened to my sister. I grabbed the knob to the kitchen door, easing it open, I did a quick check for cops, and nope, I was in the clear. They were down by the dock area.

In the distance I saw the old man and his dog get in his boat and push off from shore, they must be going fishing like they did every evening back then, even in the rain, these Bayou people, just tough old birds, I've got to say. I looked at the sky behind the boathouse, a storm was about to overtake the Bayou, a big storm. Thick black clouds and lightning with drums of thunder following, it looked like an invading army rolling in. Suddenly a heavy wave of rain blew across the Bayou, overtaking everything in its path. I saw flashlights darting everywhere for cover.

This storm is going to destroy any clues out there for sure. The officers couldn't see me standing next to the wood pile my dad built many summers ago, not that they were looking for me. For whatever reason I just shot off down the dock, stopping before I got to Sara. The rain pouring now, a cold blanket of wet falling down on all of us. I looked out on the Bayou, you could see the mist rolling in behind the wall of rain, ready to blind the Bayou in white thick mist... I turned slowly to the tree, our tree, Sara was still up there.

This would be the last time I would see my sister. My mission was clear now, my head was also very clear. I know I keep saying that, right? As I stared at the death tree, thinking someone was going to have to die and pay for what they had done!

There were two policemen at the cabin end of the dock, flashing their lights my way and yelling for me to get off the dock. As they began to run towards me, a bolt of brilliant light hit the tree, the tree where Sara was still hanging, sending it and Sara into a ball of yellow flames. The policemen now stopped in their tracks, the old man stood up in the boat, the other officers that dotted the shore line all turned to see the fireball.

In the bright flames and smoke, everyone in confusion over what to do, her body, the evidence was all but gone and I was on my way to do the same. I turned and walked past the men still staring at the fire ball. I made my way up the path to my sister's car. I looked back and blew her a kiss as the flames overtook her body, then jumped in and started the car while looking in the rear-view mirror as the death tree was burning. A peace came over me. It only lasted a second though. Sara had her burial, a burial by fire---somehow that seemed fitting for her. I sped off up the road without anyone noticing.

In the rear-view mirror, the flickering brilliant orange and yellow flames roared to the sky as my childhood memories faded with the flames of the death tree. Everything changes, for better or sometimes worse, only time will tell, tick tock, tick tock...

Good bye Sara, good bye little sister.

Chapter 7

THE OTHER SIDE OF THE MIRROR

*'Some people give themselves over to their most evil desires, and those people become evil. But in general, it's reductive to think of evil as something foreign and separate from the rest of us. Evil is part of everyone. We all have the capacity to
commit evil acts.'*

Bill James

The key worked. The old speckled glass door creaked open like a horror movie. The place was dark but had a smell of vanilla. Sara loved that smell, that sexy smell.

I stood there adjusting to the darkness. I could make out a French settee just inside the door. It had to be from the 1700's and all about French.

She loved that stuff from the little bit of time we spent together. I had to sit down, and the settee was beautifully inviting, nice Cush to it... as I ran my hand across the fabric.

I sat for a moment to catch my breath and let my mind catch up to where we are in this story. I was trying to remember a little more about our short time together. Against the opposite wall, I noticed a small table with a brown glass bowl on it and a gold framed mirror hanging above.

I could almost see my reflection in the gold framed mirror. I was afraid to look at myself. My day had been filled with a little more excitement than normal, at least for this architect. Ok, I did walk over and look into the mirror, but the eyes of the person in the mirror were dark and troubled looking, not my beautiful green hazel eyes. Part of me didn't know that person...

I couldn't look away though; those eyes captured me, as my head began to flash random thoughts of the last several hours. My hands gripped the table's edge for the ride my head was about to go on again. The flashes began at the tree this time, the fireball that took my sister away. My eyes flickering as the 3-D tour of the cabin went on, my body shaking as I stood. My knees buckled, and my eyes rolled back in my head, with my body going limp, I hit the floor in another mind orgasm like the one at the tree.

My eyes finally opened this time, I was face down on the floor with the brown bowl under my right arm and all its contents all over the floor around me. I thought about Jack. Why Jack and not Sara? He lost all the evidence the tree and my sister's body held. I hope he found the stuff I laid out for him in the cabin---as for me, I covered my tracks ok, I hope.

Thank God, Sara had a closed garage at the bottom of the apartment; well, I hope it was hers anyway. I knew I needed to get off their radar, and find this guy. I didn't really know how I was going to find him though.

"STOP AND STAY ON TASK shouted that voice... Stay focused and find her killer, no time for doubting shit, Raven," that voice in my head said.

I crawled over to the settee in the entrance and pulled myself onto it. I laid there and began to gaze over the apartment. An apartment Jack has no idea about, Jack said he had my address, but never said he had Sara's, which is good. I needed time to check this place out for information about who this guy is and who my sister was, really was. She must have left some clue to him here. This is all wildly bizarre for me.

This is her place, her sanctuary; she was so close to me too, minutes from my front door. I wondered if she already knew about me, but was afraid to come see me? This whole thing is such a damn shame, a very, very painful shame. Ok voices, I will stay here tonight, then tomorrow morning before dawn start the great fake getaway. The plan is, I will slip back to my place in an Uber, I just love the Uber.

No, no... that will leave a trail back to here---wait Sara has a bike downstairs, I saw it when I put the car in somebody's garage on the way up earlier. How could I miss that multi-colored thing with her name painted on the frame, 'Sara's Urban Machine, peddle me SUM...' Perfect, I will ride it to my place and pack some things, call to make flight arrangements for a long European trip, with no end date; then call the Partners, well, Norman, to explain my leaving---they will understand and want me to clear my head after my sister's death. I can trust Norman.

What else needs to happen---leave notes on my kitchen counter for plants and air conditioner control, that way I can leave without anyone being the wiser? I hope, right? I will need to draw some money out of the bank, I guess I need to use the ATM at the airport, and then I will take a

Uber to the airport leaving a trail of my departure. Stuff my shit in an airport locker like you see on TV, and slip back out to Sara's place to plan.

Ok, maybe that isn't going to work. I can't leave the bike at my place, Jack could figure that out in a second, and airport cameras will give me away. I need them to think I'm gone in the wind, rightfully so. What about playing dress up with some of Sara's stuff, she was the total opposite of my style. That should keep Jack off me for a while. As tense as I am now, I wouldn't mind him all over me, right… Ok then, I will change in the airport bathroom after the security check then slip back out and Uber back to the apartment. At this point I'm not a suspect anyway, right?

Wait, I should Uber to the cafe at the end of the block just in case. The fun thing behind the Uber, which is you always get an interesting driver each time, I like to talk to them and hear their story---we all have stories---look at mine so far, I'm actually evading the FBI, U.S. Marshals and local police, go figure, right...?

I must have fallen asleep as I was thinking of my day. I really needed it. Morning was about to break when I woke up on the settee, which was too small for my whole body by the way, but there I was staring at the ceiling.

 The appearance of her apartment when you walk in is a very neat clean French style for the period of the building. As you look to the left of the settee I'm lying on was the living room with an upholstered French two seat sofa and matching chair in the corner.

Behind that, sat a round ornate table with freshly cut flowers, looking kind of old and really dead now in a clear vase. There were four small chairs in a little nook. Next to the table was a very large bookcase on the wall all by itself. It sat between the nook and kitchen, which was odd---the wall was blank to the left and blank to the right. The kitchen was a little galley kitchen with just the simple essentials.

I dragged myself up and stood in the middle of the room and took a couple of glances around the place. The place had a very clean and crisp appearance, nothing out of the ordinary, except that big gaudy bookcase and the blank wall space. No mail, no papers, except the stuff in the bowl at the front door. No closet and no bed. Where did she sleep? There was nothing out of place like it was picture perfect, staged almost.

What was I missing? I noticed a little window in the kitchen, as I walked over to it and climbed up on the sink to peek out---I could see there was a terrace out there. I looked back at the room but no other openings or doors. I tried to open the window with no luck. It was painted shut. I could see the bathroom window to my right though. I climbed down from the sink and headed to the bathroom. I had to pee anyway.

I hit the latch and the window opened onto the terrace. I hung half way out the window and looked around before I began to climb out to make sure this was a good idea---like I'm full of good ideas lately--- when my shoe got stuck on a nail in the window frame. That sent me face first down to the tiled floor of the terrace. I lay there for a second, thinking about what am I doing climbing out windows; running from police and FBI; and most of all looking for a killer... really Raven, what did I think I was doing besides acting crazy?

Really though, this wasn't in the college overview, but here I was, dazed and confused. This time Jack wasn't here to pick me up from the ground like he had been doing all day yesterday. Who the hell am I? I'm confused, more confused than ever. I know back at the tree I thought I knew what to do but, not really.

I pulled myself up and took a look around. What a great terrace this was! It overlooked the streets of the French Quarter and Mississippi River. This view was breathtaking, and the sun was about to break through the morning clouds. The lights from below were beginning to pop on all over the city as I got ready for my morning. I really had to get moving-- it's getting late; I only had a little darkness left. I climbed back in the bathroom window and headed for the door. I noticed a big blue floppy hat hanging on a hook next to the door and I grabbed it as I ran out the door and headed down to the bike.

I hopped on and sped off to my place only blocks away. As I rounded the corner to my street, everything looked ok as one of the old green street cars passed my place like they do every morning, afternoon and evening. There were no strange cars anywhere; nothing seemed out of place for my street in the pre-dawn hours of a day. I rolled up to the house next door; Ms. Carolina's, she is out of the country right now, visiting her son in England. I made sure the coast was clear before I went any further.

I then rolled the bike next to my neighbor's English flower garden just over the fence on the driveway side of the house from mine. I stopped to look around once more, and everything seemed good, so I jumped the fence and let myself in the side door of my house and headed to the bedroom to grab some stuff. I pushed the crap in the suitcase and I gave myself a shot of perfume and looked for the phone, yes, I still have a land line. It came with the house, it's green and has a round dial, and is very loud when you spin that dial. Which it being a land line, is a good thing. Jack will be able to confirm my plans. I called my Uber, then the partners, well, Norman. That was hard, but they are totally behind me. Thank God!

I wrote the sticky notes and placed them all around for Jack to see. And by then, the honk of my Uber was ready. I hit the door, and locked it, for possibly the last time, what a thought.

 I rolled my suitcase down the walkway and off we sped to the airport. I took a minute and pulled the hat down over my face, then closed my eyes as we drove, the driver respected my space and didn't say a word. Once we reached the airport he dropped me curbside. I popped out and shot to the nearest overseas desk and picked up my ticket to France.

I walked over to the short line, where I stood behind a young couple with a kid in a stroller talking about their upcoming visit with Mom in France. How sweet.

 I made it through security and headed for the nearest bathroom. I hid in a stall and looked in my suitcase to see what I had to change into---nothing much, but I had the clothes Sara had on that first night she was at my place. With that blue hat I grabbed from Sara's place, they would work perfectly together. I walked out of the bathroom to the lockers just to the left and popped my case into number 124 and headed for the door. I flagged a cab and told the man 334 Royal St., Cafe Beignet in the French Quarter, just down the street from Sara's place. He knew the place and headed there, I left my hat on to cover my face and to my luck he didn't seem to speak English, so score one for me.

Thankfully traffic was light this morning, score again. We got there in less than twenty minutes, and I paid the man in cash and ran into the cafe. I ordered some brain liquid and took a sip before heading out the back entrance, which lands on Sara's street steps away from her apartment. I looked around before I ran up the steps and unlocked the door. There, I had to take another second to look in all directions once more, in every window, at all the cars; I saw no one and no shadows. Now inside, I shut the door behind me and fell back against it half expecting Jack and his team to be standing there waiting, but nothing. I just closed my eyes and slid to the floor in relief. I took in as much air as I could, thank God, I was in the clear.

I gave myself a minute before I pulled myself up and walked to the middle of the room again, remembering what I had seen last night and this morning, like the window, oh yeah. I went into the bathroom and sat to pee, then climbed out it once more, without falling this time. I sat in a lounge chair just to the left of the window and sipped the rest of my coffee. The view of the morning sky from the terrace at that hour was inspiring. With that view and the morning air stirring, I must have fallen asleep. The sounds of a trumpet playing nearby woke me. Holy shit, it was just about evening now, I had slept through the day.

The night was settling in, and the lights downtown started to flip on. I could hear some people below me in the courtyard talking as they began to gather. They lit a small fire in the stone fire pit in the middle of the courtyard that joined our buildings. I watched them for a minute, talking and laughing with one another. A couple of guys began to play music in the corner. That made me smile for a brief moment, when the vision of Sara hanging in that tree began to flash in my head sending me to my knees.

Holding my head, rocking back and forth again, I fell forward on all fours with my head on fire again, throwing up right there. The pressure in my head felt like it was splitting in two. Then flashes, flashes of Sara started popping in my head like a flash bulb going wild. I rolled around the terrace floor holding my head in pain.

Then my body started to jerk and shake, like at the tree. It was happening again, the mind orgasm. I blacked out at some point. When I opened my eyes, I was looking up into the night sky, with music playing from below and a plane was above with its lights blinking against the stars. As it flew out of sight, I sat up---wow, that sucked.

My vision still foggy, but I noticed two French doors in front of me. I crawled over to them and tried to look in; they were locked of course and lined with thick black curtains. I sat back on the terrace floor to look at the building and how it was constructed, remembering that I am an architect, after all. These doors had to be part of Sara's apartment. I jumped up and pulled at the doors trying to force them open.

They were not budging, so I went back to the window and slid my skinny ass inside and rolled right out the door of the bathroom into the living room. I stood up to look at the wall that divides the apartment. The only thing on that wall was that large bookcase. That spanned at least six feet and was floor to ceiling; it was painted the same color as the walls. It blended in really well.

There was nothing on either side of it. Not even pictures on the wall, just blank space, why?

I began pulling out books to see what was behind them, nothing but solid wood. I looked for anything that would move; I tugged and prodded all over these things, still nothing. I noticed near the top of the cases was a painted pipe that ran through the bookcases and stopped about three feet on each side near the ceiling. It was hidden by a wood flap thing built into the wall.

I jammed my fingers between the two cases and pulled as hard as I could.... They didn't budge, but I was onto something. I stood back and played with it in my architectural mind, trying to figure it out. These were built to move, I started to look for a lock or latch, some moving part or piece had to be the answer.

Well, shit---nothing. I began jerking all the books off the shelves and onto the floor. I even yelled 'open sesame' then clapped my hands twice to see if that would work. I climbed up on the small ledge to get a better look at the top and the top shelves. That's when I saw the black pull latch carved into the side panel. Snap, Snap I pulled both latches and jumped down to see what happened.

Again, I dug my fingers into the cases and pushed. They glided open to each side, making a click, clack sound as they rolled. There, I was met with thick black curtains with red, a blood red satin lining. I grabbed each panel and yanked them open. I wasn't expecting them to be that heavy, but they opened. Holy shit I'm in...

Still too dark to see much past my foot, I fumbled around for a light switch, but nothing---I used my iPhone for light as I felt my way around the room, both sides of the walls were empty, no switches. I could see small bits of light coming through something at the other end of the room. I turned to head towards the small flashes of light and I was met by a large wooden table centered in the room. I made my way past it and found the opening.

It was those French Doors that opened out to the terrace I had found from outside. I took both hands and jerked both curtain panels as hard as I could, I wasn't ready for what was behind me, as I stood in amazement, no, shock... What was all this shit?

I was in a gothic dungeon in the middle of New Orleans. I wanted to just close my eyes and get out, but I had to go all the way with this, if I was going to find what happened to Sara. This was my only lead to find that murdering son of a bitch. I took a breath and stepped forward, my eyes went right to the table in the center of the room. A ten foot solid thick, Gothic style and very heavy mahogany wood table. At the head of the table sat a lone chair...

There was a large chandelier hanging over it with candles instead of light bulbs. On the opposite side of the room, another set of black curtains hung. At the end of the table facing me was a large tapestry of something. It was too dark to make it out. I could however, make out an object hanging from the ceiling, held in the air by four chains hooked to the ceiling. What the hell, as I rubbed my temples to this bizarre discovery.

Then I noticed to my left sat a web cam on a stand, hidden caddie-corner from where I was standing, it was aimed at the table, but camouflaged within a couple of tall fake plants. Real plants couldn't live in this dark dungeon for sure. My mind was racing with all kinds of things now. I noticed little square tables along the walls on both sides all filled with candles.

You could see old wax that had melted and dripped over the sides of all the tables, forming a cascading wax waterfall to the floor. One table had a box of matches on its corner. I opened it and struck one, as I began to light the candles all around the room. The room came into focus. I was in a room right out of the Game of Thrones or something---right here in New Orleans. What a Great show by the way, very sexy.

When I finished lighting those candles, I climbed onto the top of the large dark table that took up most of the room to light the chandelier. I stood for a moment, as the other candles flickered all around me. I took in every inch of this gothic nightmare. I mean dark in every way your mind could go, every way... I didn't know whether to cry or run, run fast?

It was clear that Sara was involved in two completely different worlds---two very conflicting worlds at that---this one involving a web cam, and a lot of wax. What happened to my baby sister? I jumped down and made my way back into the living room hoping to find who my sister was---trying to take all this in, the *real* Sara. I ran my fingers across pictures, table tops. I sat in all her furniture; I touched everything and still had no clear idea. I saw the keys and CD that I laid on the floor while sitting on the settee when I came in.

"Talk to me girl, help me understand and to see who you are; what you almost told me back at the Bayou." I saw an old CD player on the shelf next to the fireplace. I laid the CD in and pushed the only button I saw. I walked to the kitchen and poured myself a glass of wine, which I needed, really needed, after what I'd found. I tipped the glass up and swallowed the whole glass, then poured another and sat down in front of the fireplace. With my free hand, I popped a log into it and struck a match. Fire began to flicker with a crackle, then warmth from the fire hit my face, I stared at the flames for a second, then two, then three... I got lost in the fire; the flames took the shape of the death tree.

The CD had slid in by itself and began to play; it played sounds of soft Celtic music, I think. Rich tones, all female, I let the sounds take me and I began to drift away which I needed right now, the wine was helping too.

The drifting landed me back in the kitchen, pouring some more wine. After I poured my glass, I looked down at the glass itself---it was more of a gothic goblet than a wine glass, "so I'm getting a little gothic tonight." I just began swaying, sliding, walking and sipping to the tunes from the CD, not my normal music but it kept my attention.

I danced throughout the apartment, rolling through the rooms, just lost, then suddenly I was in front of the dark curtains I had closed earlier. I reached up with my free hand and grabbed the curtain. I jerked the left side back and the room was exposed again. I stepped through the curtains and saw the French doors, the doors I had opened earlier; I just stood for a moment to see the lights from the city beaming up from the streets below and the whispers of New Orleans music filling its streets. These beautiful French doors leading out to her rooftop wonderland, who could ask for more than this, she was sitting on top of the life blood of the French Quarter.

I'm a little jealous as I watch all the night crawlers disappearing into the little shops, restaurants and night clubs for blocks. The music playing in clubs drifted up and filled the apartment with the sounds of jazz and blues. I reached the terrace's edge to watch the city some more. Tonight, the sky was a stark black, lit with millions of stars. They lit the city I love like fireflies.

Between the wine, the music and the city view, I was just so deep into a nice new place right now, as a song from the CD hit the speakers, 'Playing with madness'. I focused on the words, playing with madness, playing with you... They took me over all of me. I just wanted to feel this way all the time and find the creep that did this to my sister and play--- play with him as he did with my sister.

Play in madness, his madness, be a little dark and nasty myself. Those innocent days from the summers at the Bayou are now gone, just a memory. But not forgotten, never forgotten.

Chapter 8

The Puzzle

I've never been a big cinephile which may be why I could treat 'The Clock' like a puzzle and force the pieces to fit together in odd ways.

Christian Marclay

The Fire Chief cleared the area where the tree was, so Jack and the other investigators could start to look for any---anything left. Jack was not hopeful but had to try.

Oliver was over at the base of what was left of the tree when out rang screams from a local CSI, "I found something in the cabin, I need Jack now!"

The boys hit the path and headed to the cabin, Jack in the lead. He met the CSI at the cabin door, "Jack, this stuff was not here when we did the first sweep of the area. I did this cabin myself!"

Jack walked over to the display of evidence on the kitchen floor. He barked, "Has anyone seen Raven since the fire yesterday?" The room fell silent...

"Oliver, get a car to her place and try her phone. Hey, send someone to her job also." Oliver was on the radio setting everything in motion that Jack asked for. Jack dropped to his knees to go over the evidence Raven left; Sara's torn blue shirt, purse and the finger nail. Jack knew it was Raven who found the missing pieces.

He began to bark orders again, "Bag everything and get me all the prints you can. I mean finger prints, palm prints, lip and toe prints---yes, I did say lip and toe prints---anything we can get guys. I'm being serious, look for them in weird places, like just under the loft rail as if you were standing on the ladder holding on to it - think like they would - and under the rim of the table as if you were laying on top of the table and grabbing the edges, don't forget the leather straps, on the ladder and corners of the table. I want them printed also. Remember we need to get the stuff to MY lab, not local---my guys, only my guys at the FBI field office in Baton Rouge---no one else is to be trusted with this stuff!"

Oliver broke from the radio and looked over at Jack, "Are you officially taking over this case, Jack---you know what that means, right?" Jack sat back on the floor and didn't say a word, just stared at the evidence in front of him. Oliver has known Jack for years, and he knew when Jack was taking over a case. Oliver pulled out his cell phone from his pocket and called FBI agent Lizzy Collins, Jack's second in command. "Lizzy, this is Oliver, I think you had better get down here, Jack is at it again. He just hijacked my case and we both know what that means. He's got something, Lizzy."

Lizzy didn't hesitate, "We are thirty minutes out, Oliver. I have everyone here, and they are loading up now---Oliver, does he need anything?" Oliver laughed and said, "A clean shirt and drawers please, Lizzy---he hasn't stopped since yesterday." She laughed and said, "That's our boy---see you in thirty. Text me where you want us!"

Oliver walked over behind Jack and put his hand on Jack's shoulder, "What do you see, brother?"

Jack looked up and said, "This guy has been doing this shit for a while. Ollie, I feel it---this crime scene was too easy, just look how she was displayed in the tree and how all this was laid out. He is an organized killer, a very good one! Can you have your guys look for any similarities to anything like this in your area? Wait, go wide with this. Call Domingo (Special agent Domingo Alvarez---computer whiz kid on Jack's team). Have him give you our access to VICAP (The Violent Criminal Appreciation Program) to keep you off anybody's radar, and don't forget NCIC (The National Crime Information Center). "Oliver, has anyone found Raven yet?"

"Jack, we know she is in Sara's car and Raven's car is in her driveway, but she is not answering the house phone. I have men ready to go in. I can get a warrant in ten---wait, Jack, the guys I sent to her office, just called in and said they were able to talk to all partners and they all confirmed she left for Europe to clear her head---that she couldn't handle it and needed to get away--- their words, Jack."

Jack dropped his head and told Oliver that this was his fault. He made the decision to take her to the Bayou. He knew that would screw her up, but he needed answers. Not a good move on his part. Oliver got the car; Jack was pretty quiet on the way to Raven's house.

About the time Jack and Oliver rolled up to Raven's house, Lizzy, Jack's second in command, was standing in the driveway on the phone. She was making hand gestures in the air to whoever was on the other end of that call. She looked pissed about something. Jack shook his head and laughed, "Did she miss me, or did you call her Oliver?"

Oliver didn't pay any attention to Jack as he stepped out to hug Lizzy. Lizzy threw Jack a small black duffle and said "You need to clean your shit up, boss. Jack, the rest of the team are at the Bayou now---what a mess, lightning hit the tree, wow, that's messed up."

All Jack could do was smile, then said, "We wouldn't have it any other way now would we, Lizzy girl? Did you see anything in house before we got here by the way?

Lizzy walked over to Jack, "Well, she is gone, that is for sure. She made arrangements to fly out this morning at Lakefront Airport and there is no end date on the ticket. She left notes all over the place for plant care and lights--- this chick is very organized and thorough, Jack. She did pack a bag, and must have used a taxi to get to the airport. I have Domingo looking for the cab company now; EJ (Special agent Elsa Johansson) is after the tapes from Lakefront security. It's a small airport we may get lucky. We are doing everything we can at this point. Do you suspect her, Jack?"

Jack looked at Lizzy and said, "No, not at all. I don't like her out of our reach, just in case this guy decides to come after her too."

A car pulled up to the curb. It was EJ, and she had her hands full of tapes from the airport. EJ, was shaking her head as she approached Jack. "Jack, nothing---your girl went through security and flew off to wherever she was heading. I will hit the house with Domingo, and see what you guys missed, after we clear it---do you want us to set up shop here, Jack?" EJ said, as she slipped into the side door of the house, not waiting for an answer.

Jack was standing half naked in the driveway talking to Oliver and Lizzy as he changed his shirt and dabbed some deodorant on. "We need to hear from the boys in Baton Rouge, we need to know if they have anything yet."

"Jack, I'm headed back to my shop to see what my guys have found on the search for the Display Killer you asked for," said Oliver as he jumped in his car.

Jack looked at Lizzy and mumbled, "Fucked this one up---we lost the body and any evidence on it, and even the ground around it. This bastard is lucky so far."

Lizzy had that bulldog look on her face. "Jack, this was too elaborate for just a kill---first timer, no way, he has done this before. Our profile so far, has this guy as a very organized killer, and a sadist, a sexual sadist to be exact. The Display of the body tells that story. We don't know the why yet, or what his motivation is, or what gratification gets him off yet, but we will hit on something, then we will know his victimology, and be able to track him." Jack turned and headed for the house.

All the investigators and the FBI team were standing in the kitchen, when Jack and Lizzy walked in. "Ok, what do we have?" Lizzy said. EJ began to tell them that Raven's place was neat as a pin, with nothing they could use.

"Ok guys, we need to set up camp somewhere. I will call Oliver and get us a place. I'm thinking in Ascension Parish, near the murder site," Jack explained.

Lizzy turned to ask Jack a question, "Do we have an address on the victim, by the way? Why haven't we checked out her place yet, Jack?"

Jack smiled, that was two questions---and began to tell her it's a P.O. Box in the middle of the French Quarter and, to top it off, the shop keeper has no real records to go on--- "all cash"---no cameras anywhere---not even outside, and the lingering smell of pot. Oliver and his guys were there yesterday."

Domingo looked up from his computer and explained that we should stay in the city. "There were more tracks here than there---We have a P.O. Box for our victim and Raven's house. Jack knows it makes sense and his gut has been telling him that for a while now."

EJ stood up from the kitchen bar stool and began to explain, "Well, y'all, we have the address of the shop that has P.O. Boxes. Oliver says it is a stoner's haven for pot shipments. We don't actually have a number for which box is hers anyway."

Everyone in the room looked over at Jack, "Really, how can this be possible? We went through her purse, car and registration, right? Did we not get *anything*? How about Raven's stuff, she must have an address for her sister?" Jack exclaimed, as he looked at the egg yolk on the countertop that Raven was cleaning up yesterday when they were here.

Lizzy walked over to Jack, and put her hand on his shoulder, remarking, "Boss, somehow the car registration is under the P.O. Box shop's address. They are both in the wind, literally. We have nothing on Sara, and now, not even fingerprints---everything went up in flames. Your girl Raven is gone with no trace as well. We have torn this place up and nothing. All we have, Jack, are the clues from the possible killer--maybe his DNA on the shirt, but we aren't sure he is the killer or just a guy who fucked his girlfriend there in the cabin one night. Basically, we've got a dry hole, Jack."

Domingo turned his computer around to show Jack that the nearest camera to the P.O. shop was three blocks in all directions. The City had not yet put cameras in that quad yet. Domingo spoke up with, "Jack, why don't you have Lizzy and EJ go talk to the owner---you know, talk to the shop keep and all his workers to see if the ladies can jog their stoned-out memories a little."

Jack nodded with a grin..."Ladies, would you be so kind as to take the picture of Sara and Raven over there, and see what you can dig up. And Oliver, can you--I mean you and your best guy---go back to her office and see if you can find an address for Sara, something."

"Great, Boss, I'm on it." Everyone in the room stopped and turned to look at Oliver.

"Boss" you said Boss?"

"Well, this shit happens every time I work with him, every damn time. And I had better grades in college then he did...."

Well, that seemed to lighten the room a little in light of a big investigation that happened to be stalled at the moment. The team gathered their stuff and headed out in different directions to get some work done and find something, anything.

Jack stayed behind as they left. He walked back into the living room and sat on the sofa where he had sat with Raven--- he needed to reflect back on the events of the past two days. Jack slid down just a little and put a pillow behind his head while stretching his long legs out in front of him. He had his pistol in his left hand, out to his side, safety on, but ready like always. Jack made the mistake of closing his eyes, and hewas out in a second. Fast asleep, which he needed!

The whole while, Raven, his Raven, was only blocks away in the French Quarter. Raven was at this little corner fresh market grabbing some things for dinner. She was dressed to be invisible, like a total hippie, floppy hat and sunglasses, still wearing Sara's clothes from the airport get-a-way. Her own mother wouldn't have recognized her, if she had a mother. She parked the bike out front next to the steps. Raven leaned over to lock it up on the rail, when a young man whizzed by her and headed up the steps. She followed him quietly with her hands full of food.

"Excuse me, who are you and what are you doing?"

Startled, the kid jumped up and began babbling that he was the courier, and he was just doing his weekly mail run. He told me that today, he was ten minutes late with the mail. I had a puzzled look on my face, as he babbled on about how he was paid every month to bring mail here and drop it and that he was instructed to choose different times to do the drop and different days as well. He was never to do the same thing twice, and they preferred him to do it on bad weather days. He never asked why, then said, "I like the money, lady, your mail is inside, ok?"

"This kid has no idea that I'm not the person who lives here," I thought. I opened the door and set the bags in the entrance, as I picked up the mail, and looked back at the kid, and then over the three pieces he shoved through the slot before I tossed it in the bowl at the entrance with the other mail. As the mail left my hand, I saw an old realtor flyer half sticking out of the old mail as the new mail hit the bowl... I looked back at the kid, and asked, "Who pays you again?"

He shrugged his shoulder and told me, "The money is deposited in my account once a month and I just do this courier thing for a couple of people and go to school. That's all I know, lady!"

I had to press this kid, to get all I could, anything. I tried to get the address where he picks up the mail. The kid pulled a card out of his pocket and handed it to me saying "Just ask for Big Poppa, he knows the know, I guess anyway? Can I go now, lady?"

"Yes, thank you." I rushed back to the bowl and pulled out the flyer with a picture of a gorgeous man on the front, his name was Collin Strapmore, of Strapmore International Properties, and they are hosting a Gala this coming Friday night at the Monteleone Ballroom for the Lost Women of New Orleans. I stepped over to the settee and sat holding the flyer---with the date circled in pen with a smiley face drawn in, "Are you the one, are you my sister's killer?"

I laid the flyer aside for now and went to put the food away. Standing in the small kitchen I had this feeling in my gut to send this to Jack and let him run with it. A dangerous thought I know, but then he would run in that direction for a while and leave me be, this could be good.

I put that floppy hat back on, then headed for the bike down stairs. I sped down the street, headed right for my house a few blocks away. I kept an eye out for signs of any local police or the FBI. You know, strange vans or service trucks, anything out of the ordinary. I didn't need to get picked up at this point. After all, I'm in Europe right...?

I stood a block down and hid behind a grand old oak tree and watched the house, my house - so surreal, right... I left the bike at the tree and walked across the street to Ms. Carolina's front gate and went in and rounded the side of her house. Carolina wouldn't be home for at least two more weeks.

I walked over to the waist high fence between her house and mine, watching for a couple of minutes. I saw shadow figures moving around in my house, mostly in the kitchen. I hopped over the fence and stepped closer to the windows. All clear so far - I made my way to the back door and listened for any movement as they talked about the case. And as they sat in the kitchen talking, I turned the handle to ease the door open to the mud room, sliding in quietly. All good so far. I made my way to the hallway, and saw someone's head on the sofa, panicked, backed myself against the wall---but the figure didn't move, and this God-awful sound was coming from the room, someone was snoring like a bulldozer killing a mountain.

I took the first step into my living room and peaked over the top of the sofa. Jack, Jack was asleep on my sofa, really asleep. I inched my way around to the front of the sofa, and just watched him sleep for a couple of minutes. I had choices to make here, leave the flyer or wake him up---my mind was all over the place. I placed the flyer gently in his lap, just like he did with the photo of me and Sara. I paused, hoping he would wake up and see me.

That's not what I really needed at this moment; I quietly made my way to the back door and slipped out without being heard. I headed for the fence, when from behind me a car with its lights on bright, hit the driveway. I leaped and threw myself over the fence falling into the English flower bed below. I laid there just in case they heard me, then I heard the squeaking of my front door. They were inside, and I was in the clear, so I made a dash for the front gate of Ms. Carolina's and calmly walked over to the bike, the get-a-way vehicle. I looked back at the house, my house. I didn't know what my future held at this point, if I'd ever get to see the house again, but I knew I had to keep stepping forward in this adventure for Sara. I hopped on the bike and rode off into the night.

Lizzy and the team quietly walked into the living room to find Jack asleep and snoring on the sofa. Domingo whispered, "Can I tweet this?" The team all busted out laughing when Jack's eyes popped open as he sat up quickly.

The flyer Raven set in his lap had now slid in between the cushions. "How long have I been out?" Everyone just looked at each other, and didn't say a word.

 When Domingo shot out with, "I got something you didn't ask for, Boss, and I got a hit on it just now."

"Ok then, go D..." said Jack.

"SWEAT, we got some sweat! The lab pulled some DNA from the whip we sent in. It belongs to a Romanian deportee. His name is Constantine Lanculescu---he was here on a work visa---he screwed that up with a DUI charge, and then slapped a cop with a 2x4 sending the officer to the hospital and Constantine back to Romania...Funny thing is, I also pulled a U.S. Driver's license and birth certificate under the name John Gardner from New Orleans, Iberia Parish to be exact, and Jack, it's current. Iberia is next to Ascension Parish! Jack, this is the same guy. Two names, two ID's, that close to the murder site? And yes, Jack, the address is a Marina, "boats and ships. The info is on its way to your phones now."

Jack stood up and said, "Road trip, anyone?"

The crew hit the front door like it was a free food buffet. Jack was the last one to get to the SUV sitting in the driveway. Lizzy was behind the wheel, so Jack jumped in the passenger side, "Roll Lizzy, roll."

Chapter 9

PLAYING WITH MADNESS

'It's like a fever - Being with you... Is playing with madness - playing with you - playing with madness - playing with you - I feel a rush inside my veins...'

Song by Schiller

Sara's music, that song---'playing with madness', was drawing me back in the apartment. It's time to explore my sister's life some more. I don't know who she became after all these years, but something inside was driving me to let this adventure continue. Who was I kidding, I had to---I wouldn't stop until I got all my answers, anyway!" I am playing with madness now, my madness!

I stepped back in from the terrace, walked past the hidden camera to that large Gothic dining room table sitting dead center in the room. I noticed near the middle of the table were dots of shiny wax droppings from an antique metal chandler hanging above the table, with candles instead of light bulbs, very romantic in a normal reality, definitely not in this one.

I saw several colors of wax dotted around the table almost in a same sort of a pattern at the cabin. I pulled back the chair, the heavy Gothic thrown chair, and then sat myself down, gripping the ends of the arms, that were carved into lion's paws. I gripped them tight, really tight---until all the blood had vanished from my hands, before letting go. I held my hands, my shaky hands, over the table for a second or two then placed them on the top of the table running them back and forth across the old wood.

I noticed ties on each corner leg of the table just under the table top; they were woven leather strips, again like the cabin. My mind was trying to grasp what all this meant, but down deep, I already knew what this meant, and what she did, but I didn't know why.

Then, from the corner of my eye, was the hidden camera. The picture was beginning to come clearer now. My sister had her own following of sorts. How could someone fall so deep into a world such as this?

I pushed away from the table and walked around the table with my hand brushing the surface as I walked. I reached the chair again, the only chair at the table. The rest of them were placed against the walls on all sides. I stepped up on the chair, and then took another step up onto the table, to see it from above. This felt like a stage, her stage, where she was the master or maybe the toy---maybe in this world, Sara found a way to take back her control.

It was clear, the same outline as the table from the cabin, an outline of a body with the many-colored wax dots and leather straps. Displayed for all to see---on camera and in person, as they sat and watched the show.

What show was it? And who were they...?

I stood there for a couple more seconds thinking, with the hypnotic music in the background. I just felt like I had to unbutton my shirt, then I tossed it on the floor and my jeans were next, I stopped for a moment noticing my breathing was heavy. I had pressure throbbing in my temples. I felt excitement taking over inside me.

I then un-hooked my bra and dropped it in the chair as I knelt down on the table and crawled to the center. There I laid myself down under the chandler placing my body inside the pattern. I laid there looking up at the burning candles. The flickering flames were hypnotic, as my mind began to run wild with thoughts of the straps around my ankles and hands, a little drop of hot wax dripped from above landing on my nipple, sending shivers through my body.

I closed my eyes to enjoy the strange erotic sensation, only to see Sara, standing in that swing at the Bayou with the chains wrapped around her wrists, rocking back and forth. I opened my eyes just in time for a drop of hot wax to hit me on my thigh, sending me into a deep orgasm, as my back arched, and my body began slowly thrashing on the table. Wow, was this hot... I opened my eyes to see Sara above me, facing me, naked like me, having an orgasm like me, and as she smiled; she spoke one word, 'VENGEANCE' as a dot of hot wax hit me between the eyes sending me into a volley of visions of Sara, Jack and the Bayou.

The flashes grew stronger and faster. I saw her, Sara, lying there with the room full of shadow people, all with black capes on. Their faces covered with faceless masks. They all circled the table. At the head of the table was a figure sitting in the chair, but this figure wore a red cape and hood, not black like the rest of the room. Was it that guy, Collin, from the flyer? Was he behind all this? Is he the one that got her into this world and then killed her when he was done playing with her? Is this how the game works? Or did this start many summers ago? Or was this just a bad Tom Cruise movie? I know this is New Orleans, and it's a culture baked with weird after all.

I opened my eyes to see two drops of hot wax falling from above, the first hit me on my cheek, the other landing on my chest sending me off again. I began rocking while more wax began to hit my body all over. My mind was like a camera flash going off repeatedly in my eyes. The shaking started, the wrenching of my body---the mind orgasm was taking over.

Intense this time, I think I may have had a second orgasm while my mind was freaking out as well. The mind orgasms are getting stronger each time now. My mind went to all the dark places it could---it had a lot to choose from. From Sara's body hanging there for all to see, to the tree on fire; to the blood pool at the base of the tree; to her blood swirling in the Bayou; to the Bayou itself; to how run down the Bayou had become; to Jack and his beautiful eyes. Yes, his eyes, eating me up; then his shy kindness; to the fire ball from the sky; then my cabin.

I don't know how to explain it, but I'm a different person after each of the mind orgasms, I believe I have found the way to tap into my strength, my power, and how to switch it on and off. Mary called it triggers, in therapy; triggers were what set off the bad things in a person's life, so you develop things to stay clear of them. For me, I need to nurture my triggers and run towards them; or could this be that lucid dreaming stuff, Mary's explanation is a lucid dream, a dream during which the dreamer is aware of dreaming.

During lucid dreaming, the dreamer may be able to exert some degree of control over the dream characters, narrative, and environment. It's almost like I'm dealing with two people---oh shit, that's bad, I read somewhere, but I'm no expert, just a Google it queen like most women.

That power it holds, to turn it on or off, at will, now that intrigues me, my sister seemed to be a little freaky in this area, with everything I have seen so far... Wow, this double life thing she was into!

I know I only had her for a few days, but would have never guessed this, making money doing adult webcam and live shows here and at the cabin.

It just goes to show you, that anyone, any person out there, can live behind a Masquerade, a white mask and a black mask living inside you all the time... Sara had her sweet hippie thing going, and then behind closed doors, or curtains in this case, she was Mistress Annie or whatever she called herself. Look at me, I'm discovering I'm two people myself--except one of mine, is going find and kill someone. Mary, Mary quite contrary---what would you make of this...?

Jack is no dummy---they will put the pieces together soon enough. But I'm the one with the head start and I did give him the clues from the cabin and that flyer of Collin. It's like we are working together towards the same end---oh wait, he has a badge and I'm just a killer. I rolled off the table to pick up my clothes. As I slid my jeans back on, I lost my footing and grabbed the large tapestry on the far end wall, it was really beautiful. The image was something I have seen before, somewhere here in the city.

Still standing topless, and sipping my wine as I explored the image, I remembered it from somewhere; it was maybe about three years ago at Mardi Gras in a window of a gallery over on Bourbon Street maybe—yes, that had to be it - The Garden of Earthly Delights by Hieronymus Bosch. A friend from work was with me and she said she had done a paper on it back in college; she described it as teeming with a certain adolescent sexual curiosity. She said the professor was all over her about it, and yes, she did, do the professor... Was it the original? The images on the tapestry are very much in line with Sara's life as I studied it deeper. If it was the original, why and how did my sister have it here? I will chalk this one up as a clue and check out the gallery later.

I continued to walk the room, putting all these pieces together in my mind. I stopped in front of a purple painted door with a splash of deep red, washed into the middle of it. The door blended with the wall, it was almost invisible except for a knob, a black and very thick dungeon like knob. My guess, this is the bedroom, her secret place, compared to the dining room, what was I thinking, secret place---this whole place was a secret place!

I pushed on the door, entering her bedroom. It was as black in there as the dining room was, and the curtains were closed. I reached around for a light switch, but nothing; I could make out a box of matches on the dresser just inside. I struck one and began to light all the candles in the room to see how this adventure would continue.

The center piece, of course, was the king-sized bed made from thick wood, painted black. It hung dead center, floating from the ceiling on chains, yep, that's what I said, chains... I pushed on it just to see. I had to, right? It rocked back and forth, with little creepy creaks and squeaks. The chillies were back, tingling, shooting all over my body...

At the foot of the bed in the corner was a very large framed mirror, sitting on the floor and touching the ceiling. You could see the whole room looking back at you from the bed. To the right of the bed next to the dresser was a plump black leather chair. I reluctantly sat down on the edge of it for a moment, to take in the room, the whole room.

The windows were covered in the same thick curtains as the dining room, those black and blood red puppies didn't let any light in, and must be a sound barrier, as no music from the city was drifting through either.

 Between the flickers of candlelight, I could make out another door just to the right of the mirror. I swung the door open and stepped into a Gothic dream, to say the least.

The room was dark in color, with gold crackling up and down the walls. A large brass chandelier hung above the tub, candles filled its metal squiggles like the one in the dining room or play room---Sara's office of sorts. This place brings on the strange for sure, let me tell you what.

The black polished tub, French in design, sat long ways in front of the only window in the room. The tub was flanked by a small ornate dressing table with a mirror to its right. To the left was a floor to ceiling mirror framed in a thick black wood, it was cornered to give the person in the tub a mirror image of one self. Very sexy, I was getting a little hot, I must say... Wow, a rush of heat passed through me.

I noticed I was gripping the brass piping coming out of the floor at the foot of the claw foot tub; the tub had a raised back almost like one of those lounge chairs you see in the movies---the old movies from the Twenties and Thirties, right? As I gripped the pipes and the heat filled my body, I wanted to fill it with steaming hot water and bubbles of course, and lose myself in it for hours and hours.

I had been so caught up in the tub, that I didn't notice the chair sitting behind me, the old French purple parlor chair sitting alone, about three feet in front of an armoire. The chair was just sitting there, but why--it was out of place. What am I saying? This entire place is out of place!

So, I followed the strange, and sat in the chair and checked out the armoire. It was as ornate as the rest of the room, of course. The large armoire sat flat on the wall with potted plants on each side to complete the wall. I had to open the thing, of course I did! I popped myself out of the chair and pulled at the brass handles, and a gush of vanilla scented air hit my face. What stood before me was a room full of dresses, sun dresses, evening dresses, all different lengths and colors; hats, sandals, and small purses---nothing out of the ordinary.

I stepped back and fell into the chair again. I sat studying all the dresses, nothing strange or Gothic. I pulled myself up and began to run my hands through her clothes, stirring up the perfume on them. Vanilla began to surround me, I knelt in front of the armoire looking at her shoes, and as I did I could feel a draft hitting me in the face. I stood up again, to get a better look at the armoire itself. I ran my hands all around the wooden frame---noticing a split in the top molding and again in the base molding as well, the split ran from front to back.

I sat in the chair again, this time studying the armoire and the wall it sat on. Being an architect sure comes in handy with all this mysterious stuff.

The walls to both sides were solid from top to bottom, with potted plants in each corner. I needed a different view of the structure to get an idea of what I was working with. I got up and went into the dining room to see if I could see the wall from that side. There was definitely more wall length, about six feet to be exact.

Just to be sure I went outside to the terrace and followed the wall. It wasn't connected to any other apartment, so I headed back to the bathroom to find the mysterious passage into the unknown. I had no idea what I would find, but, the room was hidden for some reason, after all!

Chapter 10

Dress-Up to a Discovery

'I'm on the hunt for who I've not yet become'

Unknown

I stood in the doorway for a while and just looked, then sat in the chair and looked some more. What was behind there? I saw no pipe rail thing, like the one in the living room. No paint scrapes anywhere---a mystery. I sat back in the chair and daydreamed a little, how could I not, after all? I have really fallen into a nightmare. Day dreaming, well, architecturally day dreaming that is, and looking at all the ways this box could open.

The armoire was 5 feet plus wide, and floor to just about the ceiling tall. That's it, I believe I've got the answer. The doors are not the real doors--- well, they are doors for the front part of the armoire where her dresses and shoes are, but you don't just pull open the armoire doors, you grab the handles and push them apart, the whole thing is on large piano hinges along the rear panel on the sides. That made each half of the armoire fold back against the wall. Giving a full five foot opening to the hidden mystery---a closet of sorts, as it turns out.

I stepped in slowly to take all this in. It was almost a brain overload. Her hidden closet is the entrance to an elaborate dress-up playground, fit with everything one could want or need for a life in the New Orleans underground of pain and submission---such naughty evil. She had a wall of wigs, long, short, red, black, and a wall of, well--- bras, panties, stockings, corsets, high heels, tight leather dresses, pants, tops and then another wall with chains, whips, things I have no idea of how to use or where the things would go. Maybe I will Google a couple of them.

In the rear of this hidden room was a full-length mirror and makeup table, with a chair-stool like thing, the kind you would see in an actor's dressing room. Everything was very well done. The workmanship in here was high quality. I walked over and sat in the chair-stool and began to spin, circle after circle until I got dizzy, drunk with curiosity. This was her place, the place where Sara lived, a life most would not understand or agree with---

maybe I'm wrong with the way our society is heading today, and after all, this is New Orleans...

After my spinning in the chair, I could make out the edge of that beautiful tub; it was so---calling my name. I turned the water on as far and hot as it would go; the steam began to fill the room. Over to the side of the tub was a metal basket of all kinds of bath salts. I found the vanilla and poured it in. Oh, how I love that smell. I began to sway back and forth with the music from the street; my clothes just began to fall off me as I moved to the music. Totally naked and holding my wine glass.

I slipped one leg in and then the other, stood for a moment to let the hot water surround my legs before I began to lower myself slowly into the vanilla steam. Once I was all the way in, I leaned back and slid down until my chin touched the water. The music seemed more alive now, and it was taking me away to a relaxed place, a place where no one could touch me---my magic place.

I could feel the other me surfacing now; that person that defied the FBI. After all I did stage an uprising back at the Bayou crime scene, right? With the music flowing and another sip of my wine I slid my head under the water to drown out everything, except the evil that was playing in my head. I pushed myself up to the surface to sip more wine and plan my next move. I watched the window, as it filled with curls of stream and I could physically feel the music fill the room now. Ok, I'm a little drunk. I began to focus on Collin and who he was, who he was with, where he was, what he was doing to someone and how to find him.

He's a killer---I need to think like him, I need to see what my new selfhood can do, if I am worthy of the task, the task of killing this murderer---can I do it? It was time for a test, a test of my ability to function in their world, after all, it's my new world now... I told myself, at least for this little project, Project Collin. I stood up in front of the window, wondering if anyone could see me---it was a little exciting, all naked and stuff.

I stepped out and walked into Sara's play store of Gothic exotica, grabbing black panties, black bra, black stockings, and this black knee length leather---tight dress that zipped up the back, and had silver buckles down the front. I found a pair of black heels, spiked heels, and they fit perfectly. Painted my fingernails and toenails black, found Sara's jewelry wall, and adorned my wrists with chains and fingers with silver rings for the part I'd be playing tonight. Time for the face, a face for my dress rehearsal of power and evil...

The wig---I can't forget the wig---she has so many to choose from. I reached for the white straight hair one with fading black tips. No hesitation, it was right for tonight! I smeared on the pale white base and blacked my eyes out and blacked my lips as well, and found a silver lip cuff for my bottom lip... What a sight I was, A Gothic Queen, right...?

I headed to the foyer where the bowl was sitting at the entrance. I remembered a card stuck in the mirror---it was for a car company. I picked up her phone from its cradle and dialed the number; the voice on the other end didn't hesitate---just said a car was on its way, and hung up. I held the phone for a second, puzzled! This should be intriguing. About five minutes later a beep sounded down stairs. As I stepped out on the street, a very large black man stood at the curb holding the door open for me. He introduced himself as Jean-Paul. He was dressed in a very nice tailored suit, much to my surprise by the way---I don't know why that was, maybe because I'm used to Uber, but anyway I smiled as I slid into the back seat. He shut the door and jumped in the front seat.

"Where are we to go, ma'am?" He said with an accent, an island accent for sure.

"I'm not sure; I want a club, an underground Gothic club, a naughty club, a dark club!" I said confidently without hesitation.

"Ma'am, I know many to show you, but I think I know which you are looking for, ma'am." His English was ok in a broken island way.

Mr. Cabby took off, heading into the night and the downtown streets of New Orleans. He kept looking back at me from the rearview mirror. I finally said, "Jean-Paul, can I help you?" He jerked his eyes back to the road. He didn't say a word or glance back again.

 Then finally he spoke up and said, "Sorry ma'am, it's just that you are not the normal lady I pick up at that address." Jean-Paul turned, looking back at Raven, as his eyes narrowed in on her.

"Jean-Paul, tell me about her, that lady?" He sat quietly looking at me, not saying a thing---for all I knew the car was part of her other life, and this might not end well for me... I don't know what the hell I am getting myself into here. If I can get him to start talking maybe I can get some answers?

"Have you lived here long, Jean-Paul?" I still got no reply from Mr. Cabby. Nothing came, not even a glance in the mirror. I needed to take control before I ended up like Sara.

"Ok Mr. Cabby, have I said something or done something to offend you?"

"No, ma'am, it's just that I got to know Ms. Sara. I have been her driver for two years now, and she is very nice and respectful to me. Then you called, and she wasn't there. I don't know what to think about you---you called from her phone. We log in numbers at the depot and they call me, only me to come get her," Jean-Paul explained.

"Who are 'they', Jean-Paul?"

"I really don't know, ma'am. It's not my dispatcher, and it's another number that calls. I do know that my check is bigger driving Vulpea, than any other call, plus she tips me personally, very, very well."

"Vulpea, what does that mean? And where did you take her? Was it always the same place or different places?" I asked.

"We are here, ma'am, Club Vaudou. Do you want me to wait for you?" Jean-Paul asked.

"Jean-Paul, what does Vulpea mean? You have to tell me!" asked Raven sharply... Jean-Paul looked at her in the mirror and said the word "Fox, it means little Fox in Romanian," he said softly. We both sat quietly for a minute or two, as I decided what to say next. I looked out the window and realized we were in a less than nice place.

The buildings looked like an old warehouse in an alley off North Peters St.--- not a place for a club... more like meat packing or produce. Mr. Cabby turned down another alley and pulled up to a set of steps that led to a large steel sliding door with a man, a very large man, standing in the shadows. Jean-Paul stepped out and opened the door for me, and as I stepped out, he gently took my hand then whispered in my ear, "The password to get in is *Good Evening, Mr. Pierre,* which is the only way you will get through that door. Act like you own the place, and try to be mysterious and sexy. Ma'am, let me walk you in tonight, so you are safe."

I could see he was truly concerned, it was all over his face, and he had lifted both his hands up on my shoulders now.

"Please," he said, one last time.

"I will be fine, here, take this and wait for me." I had handed him a hundred dollar bill and wrote my cell number on the top of it. I tapped my finger on the number and said, wait for my call, then come fast! I stepped away and took the first step up to the club door. I had no idea what I was getting into and no idea what I was doing either.

Then from out of the shadows came the large black door man dressed in a black suit with a black shirt and blood red tie. His hands were folded in front of him. Like a funeral director, creepy.

He gave me the up and down, then asked, "Ka mwah edew" in broken Creole. I replied with "Good evening, Mr. Pierre" and smiled. The very large man stood looking at me, saying nothing---I thought I blew it, but he gave me a big smile with his mouth of gold teeth, I mean all of them were gold, what a sight, his hand reached for the numbered key pad and I heard a loud click and the door began to slide open slowly.

Music began to flow out of the opening. I stepped forward and as I entered, the song, Sous Le Ciel De Paris was playing. I remembered my French, thank God---the song means under the sky of Paris. I did a summer there studying architecture before graduating and remembered some. The hall was lined with people and filled with smoke, foggy smoke.

 I noticed they were all kissing and groping each other as I walked through. The people at the end of the hallway entrance were watching something. I got to the end of the hall and walked into the opening---the room was huge with a bar on the left wall next to a set of bathrooms and a dance floor in the middle. A large stage was along the back wall, and on the right side were booths with sofas and chairs---must be the VIP area...

On the stage there were people dancing to the music. I noticed tables and stools along the walls and into the main floor area. I made my way to the bar just left of the stage. I didn't make eye contact with anyone. I yelled to the bartender, "Bloody Grey Goose." He looked at me like I was mad. I smiled at him and motioned for him to come to me, and he moved my way without hesitating.

I leaned in across the bar and grabbed the dog collar around his neck and pulled hard---I pushed his head flat on the bar to whisper in his ear "Grey Goose Vodka with a splash of tomato juice, not a Bloody Mary. You will serve it to me in a high ball glass with no garnish, shaken like a Martini, I like mine chilled."

I leaned in and gave his ear a little nibble before letting go of the collar, and as he lifted his head, he had a big smile on his face, and bowed his head to me as he stepped back and began to make my drink. I watched his every move, watching to make sure he didn't put a little extra something in my drink, if you know what I mean. A girl can't be too careful in a place like this, right...?

He slid the drink my way and smiled again, then licked his lips and bowed to me again. I put a hundred on the edge of the bar and made a circle in the air with my index finger as I walked over to a table in the corner, a nice and dark spot, so not to draw attention to myself, but I think that's too late. I slid onto the bar stool that let me see the stage and most of the room as well. Within a couple of minutes, a woman, no, a girl, maybe eighteen if that, walked up and said she liked how I ordered my drinks. She had never seen it done that way before, and she came here all the time. She slowly slid onto the other bar stool.

I gave her a half smile and asked her name, she told me it was Gin---they call me Gin Gin around here---I asked why, she said because they like to sip on me slowly, like a Sloe Gin Fizz, and I leave you with a long hangover baby! I lifted my eye brow and gave her another half smile. I then asked who 'they' were. She returned my half smile and told me anyone that piqued her interest. She winked and said that I piqued her interest at the moment…

I leaned in, my lips touching her ear and whispered, "am I piquing your interest at the moment, Gin...?" I felt her shiver as I pulled away. Gin Gin took a sip, her lips were quivering as she drank, and then she smiled, as she stood up and walked over to me, she took my hand and guided me onto the small dance floor.

We danced for a while, she would slide up close then move away, then she slid up behind me and well, you can guess... I wasn't really into that, so I whipped her around and took control... I can't tell you how nice it was to break free for a couple of moments and let my guard down. That didn't last long. I noticed we were getting a lot of attention from the boys in the club, and I remembered why I was here. I slapped Gin on the ass and walked back to the table. Gin Gin stayed out there alone dancing, but not for long, guy after guy tried to join her, but she had a way of letting them know she wasn't interested. Then I noticed a group of men to my right sitting in the VIP seating. They were being waited on hand and foot... I sipped my Bloody and watched, as they pointed to Gin Gin and one motioned for a guy to go and get her. The guy was again large and black with a visible gun tucked in his pants. He walked past all the other people on the dance floor and grabbed Gin by the arm. She tried to pull away, but he was too strong, too big.

The big guy sat her down next to the greasy looking man with a lot of gold on, fingers, neck and I wouldn't be surprised if his teeth weren't all gold too. These guys had a different flare to them. Then the two black bodyguards on each side of the booth--- they were from here, but these other guys looked European, I think. I was too far away to pick up on what they were saying. The leader greasy guy handed Gin a glass of something---I wanted to go help her, but I didn't think that was a wise move.

I had to do something---as he would talk, she would look over at me---her expression wasn't a good one. At that point I headed for the restroom. I noticed one of the big guys heading my way. I went in and shut myself in a stall; I placed hands on each side of the stall and began to think of Sara, hanging in the tree.

Then I saw the blood pool in the Bayou water, the shaking started, my breathing got faster, my legs were getting weak and the flashes were popping in my head now---the whole crime scene, the words from Jack, the fire, the bolt of lightning engulfing the tree and Sara's body.

I fell back on the toilet and sat. I opened my eyes as someone began banging on the stall door---with his last knock, I kicked it open and kicked him in the balls, sending him down onto the restroom floor. He gave out a groan, as he began to lift himself. I grabbed the back toilet-seat cover, and slammed it across the back of his head and down he went. I knelt next to him and grabbed his gun and slid it in the top of my stockings, then looked for his wallet, but all he had was a passport---a Romanian passport, ok, not what I expected but I had to move quickly so I slid it under my tight leather corset top and stroked the back of his head, telling him to sleep now... Then made my way to the door. I stopped and opened it just enough to see out, the coast was clear, and out I popped. As I passed the bar I motioned to the bartender with my finger and he bowed---I made it back to my table without the Romanians noticing yet.

The bartender made my drink and brought it over to me himself. I grabbed his collar and pulled him close, then licked his neck along the base, up to his ear and asked him who were the greasy guys in VIP?

He whispered back, "Bad news, Romanian mob or something like that. They control this place, don't own it, but control it."

I asked if Gin Gin was going to be ok, and he looked up at me and said, "She is one of their pets, and she will be fine! You, on the other hand, I don't know? Gin Gin was testing you for them---by the way, you passed." I was taken aback by that, but again I didn't know this world or how it worked.

Chapter 11

Enigma

Each person is an enigma. You're a puzzle not only to yourself but also to everyone else, and the great mystery of our time is how we penetrate this puzzle.

Theodore Zeldin

My bartender friend turned to leave, and there stood Mr. Greasy himself-- no bodyguards, just him. This should be fun, I thought. My friend said, "Good lucky Chickie,," as he made his way back the bar. The creep stepped in close and told me I was interesting to him. I leaned in and began to rub my nose up and down his sweaty neck, a drop of his sweat trickled onto my lips. I could taste the salt. I eased back and lick my lips slowly in front of him, getting his attention while at the same time, I took his balls in my hand, and he began to smile, of course... I cinched down hard and gave them a twist to the left, watching the weakness take over his face...

I leaned in again, this time to whisper in his ear, "I'm going to let you live tonight, tonight you're very lucky, unlike your bodyguard in the bathroom!"

Mr. Greasy began to sink to the floor in pain as my grip grew tighter. Before he could sink any further, I leaned down and grabbed his ear with my teeth, hard enough to pop his ear lobe, spilling blood down his neck. I could hear him moan in pain. I stepped back looking down at him while I licked the blood---his blood---off my chin.

It was a wicked feeling, to see and feel how weak they really are, men that is... How easy it was to make him do whatever I wanted him to do. This was total power in my little hands. I let go of his balls at that point sending him to the floor then planted a kiss on his forehead as I headed for the door. My work here was done for the night-- test over...passed!

The sexy black hulk of a door man held the door for me as I stepped out into the night. I believe I heard him say, "Nice job", as I passed by.

I stopped just outside the front door at the railing and looked down the alley at the lit lamps along the other warehouses just off Peters Street. It was the time the thick mist from the Mississippi started rolling around the streets now. The air had a new freshness tonight, I even heard a fog horn sound from a barge, and it was loud and sounded close. I watched Mr. Cabby jump in the car, as I stepped down onto the sidewalk below to meet him, when the front door of the club behind me burst open, and out flew Mr. Greasy. He had a little limp as he held his crotch. He flew down the steps. I no sooner turned my head, when he shoved me against the red Maserati parked in front of the club. He had his left arm at my neck, while holding a knife in his right hand, high in the air ready to strike.

He was spitting words as he tried to talk, but he had such a thick accent, all I could make out was "You bitch, I will fu... , " I didn't wait for him to finish, I thrust my knee into his boys again and watched his eyes bug out of his head, then swung my arms under his and thrust upward sending both my hands into his throat, as he began to fall backwards towards the concrete sidewalk.

I reached up for his knife hand and grabbed his wrist, then drove the knife deep into his opposite shoulder. I thrust it in so hard, part of the handle went in. I gave it an extra wiggle for the heck of it. I'll bet that hurt a little.

At that moment, when the knife entered him, it sent chilly shivers up my spine, and tingling sensations all over my body. I watched him just slump to the sidewalk as I stood over him, looking at what I had done. That feeling of power came over me again. The shivers came rushing back.

When from my left side a hand grabbed my arm and pushed me to the right, it was Jean-Paul-- he was screaming in Haitian as he wielded a .38 special in the air; at the men that began to come out of the club... It was about to get crazy out here!

He looked over at me and yelled, "Come, we must get you out of here, come now!" He kept saying, "Come now, come now...", as he shuffled me into the backseat of his black sedan.

He kept the gun focused on the men from the club as he jumped in the front and sped off into the night. I sat back in my seat satisfied with my evening. I closed my eyes, reflecting on what I had done, and a sudden flash of Sara filled my thoughts. This time the flash was different, it was before she was murdered, she was looking at me with a smile on her face. I tried to piece the thoughts together and figure out what she was trying to tell me, when Jean-Paul began talking, "You need food. After such an evening you must eat. By the way, you handled him like yesterday's garbage," he said with a beaming smile.

"Food, Yes, I believe I could eat something. Jean-Paul. Let's go somewhere local, somewhere with local flair, food, and fun?"

Laughing, he remarked, "You have had enough fun for tonight. Let us just break some bread and enjoy what's left of the evening." Jean-Paul was still laughing as he shot through the mist from the Mississippi that was spilling into the streets of New Orleans.

Jean-Paul came to a stop in front of a corner store, named Verti Marte on Royal Street, near the middle of the French Quarter. It didn't look like much at all, with its weathered green half glass doors that had a half moon glass above them covered in black steel bars, typical old New Orleans. Next to the front doors was a window of equal size and color to the doors, where two chairs and small table sat. There is nothing else, very indescribable, very simple. Jean-Paul opened my car door and extended his hand with a, "Madam."

"Why yes, kind sir." I replied in a playful tone. I stepped up on the sidewalk and looked around just out of habit. I knew we were in the clear, but I still had those little hairs standing up, on the back of my neck...

Jean-Paul was at the deli door, holding it open for me, as he scanned the street. As I walked in, I noticed every eye in the place turned and looked. I must have been a sight, after all, dressed in my all black leather outfit and white straight hair from my sister's collection. We can't forget my black fingernails, lips, and blacked out eyes with a powder white face, standing in the middle of a local deli.

I had forgotten I was dressed this way. What a fun night this had been. I really have exited my comfort zone in all kinds of ways—Mary, my Therapist, would be proud of me. Well, I'm not sure she would understand the knife in the guy's shoulder part, which sent me into an almost orgasmic state, or the guy in the bathroom.

Anyway, I looked in the cases with all the yummy food. When I noticed Jean-Paul talking to the young man behind the counter in what sounded like French-Creole, he was ordering for us, I think? Then he turned to me and said, "This is my baby brother, Maximus. He will make us delicious food from my country. Come let us sit out front and enjoy the night."

I followed Jean-Paul out to the chairs in front of the window. He sat down next to me, and pulled out a cigar, motioned to me, asking if it was ok to light it and I nodded, ok. The smell was a soft pleasant one, I didn't mind it. We didn't say anything to one another just sat quietly and felt the night. I could hear music from a nearby club, and it sounded like jazz. Maximus popped out of the store carrying a tray of all kinds of different ethnic foods. He set the tray on the small table between us.

Jean-Paul began explaining what everything on the tray was; Maximus had cut all the goodies into small pieces for me to try. As we began to enjoy ourselves, we noticed every few seconds, a screaming police car would race by, heading in the club's direction. Jean-Paul would smile and glance over at me and shrug his shoulders. I just smiled back and took a bite of whatever he had just handed me.

I could tell he liked my sister, in a good way. I wanted to tell him she was my sister, but I'm not a hundred percent yet, he still could be a bad guy or an undercover cop for all I knew. I wondered if he had brought her here. She would have loved these treats from his homeland. I was actually starving after my little tangle with Mr. Greasy Romanian man back at the club. Oh, look, there goes an ambulance heading in the direction of Peters Street.

"Did you crank his nuts that hard?" Jean-Paul asked.

"No, it was the knife I jabbed in his shoulder, maybe it hit his heart, or a lung, you know something important. Besides someone like that doesn't have a heart anyway, right?" As I took a bite out of something yummy. I really had no remorse for what I had done, none at all.

"You have spirit, I like you," Jean-Paul said as he nodded his head while he ate. I sat back and took a sip of my water and looked over at him and decided to just let it out. "She was my sister---Sara was my sister, Jean-Paul."

He just stopped and laid his sandwich down looking out into the street, saying nothing. I could see tears begin to fall from his eyes, as he turned to me and said, "You used the word 'was', that's not good---I drove her home that last night, she wasn't happy, like normal, she wouldn't talk to me. We always talked. She just told me to take her to the Bayou. Then not another word---there was a man there waiting as we pulled in. This wasn't the normal; no one has ever met us at one of her stops before."

"I'd never seen him before. He came right up to my window, and handed me a hundred dollar bill and said he would see to it she got home. I watched Sara walk down to that cabin near the water. At one point she stopped and waved to me, that was the last time I saw her---I never got another call from her number until you. I knew something was wrong that night but, I didn't know what to do or who to notify. I'm not legally here in the U.S.. I have to be careful, I'm not a bad man, but I need to be careful. Do you understand?"

"Jean-Paul, it's ok---I understand completely---you're not a bad man, I can see that. If I show you a picture, would you recognize the man, would you?" I asked.

"I would like to try, please let me help, please." said Jean-Paul in a strong voice. I jumped up and said, "Get the car; I will pay your brother for the food." Jean-Paul grabbed my hand and said family don't pay---you are family now. Sister of Sara, is family now!"

As we ran to the car, I yelled, "My name is Raven." He smiled and jumped in and started the car. I told him to drive back to Sara's, and off we sped.

 We didn't say much to one another as we raced through the empty streets of the French Quarter. It is usually pretty empty at this hour of the morning, except for occasional late party goers trying to find their way home. I asked him to park in the alley behind the apartment, and we would walk through the alley to the back steps. I didn't want to chance Jack and crew being out front waiting. Little did I know, Jack wasn't who I needed to worry about.

As we approached the gate, I looked through the wood slats while Mr. Cabby tapped me on the shoulder and told me the coast was clear. I could see his 6 foot plus body had no trouble seeing over the 5 foot gate and then some. We headed up the steps to the apartment. I kept looking back to make sure we weren't being watched. It's just a habit I have now. Looking over my shoulder is second nature to me since this adventure started back at the Bayou. I now watch for figures following me in windows as I would pass, and take extra time to not take the same routes anymore---you know all that spy shit you see in movies---I figure it keeps me safe and ahead of the FBI, and the Mob I guess. I don't need them in my way on this adventure to a kill...

I opened the door and went straight to the bowl on the table and grabbed the other flyer I saved. I held it up for Jean-Paul to see. He looked at it, but it was dark in the foyer. I handed the flyer to him, so I could turn on the light for him---at that moment, I saw the expression on Jean-Paul's face---it was clear, Collin was the man that he saw that night.

Jean-Paul was visibly angry. He fell to his knees; I know he felt responsible for her. I took the flyer from his hand and asked him to sit with me on the settee. We just sat quietly for a while collecting our thoughts. I asked him if I could get him a drink or anything. He just nodded.

I poured two glasses of scotch, which we both took in one swallow... as I stood in front of Jean-Paul, I told him, I needed him to hear what I was saying. I told him I will take care of this, it is not your fault. She was into this way before him---you must trust me, do you understand, Jean-Paul? I'm going to need you later, and I have a plan to take care of all this, and I just need to know you will be there for me, ok? This means you can't go after him, you must stay away and wait for me to get things in order, and we don't know for sure if he is the one who killed her, understand?

"I will respect your wishes." He left shortly after that, and I hit the bed like a stone. I woke about 4am and lay there thinking, thinking of what I had done, going over the events of last night---I really jabbed a knife into that creep, and took a toilet lid to the other guy's head... Wow, I didn't think twice, I guess my crazy is working pretty well! I can't wait for the party tonight, Collins party...

Chapter 12

Mr. Perfect and The Hunt

Hunting forces a person to endure, to master themselves, even to truly get to know the wild environment.

Donald Trump, Jr.

Collin Strapmore, the second I saw this man, I knew---my whole body knew---he was the man---the murderer. He killed my sister. I had no doubts, but I had to prove it now---no, not really, I just had to kill him, right? Something else, as I watched this man, I could see faces, faces of women, lots of different women, young, old, white, Latin, blonde, red headed---just a lot of women flashing through my head. I had never had visions like these before. I stayed in the back and just watched. I made no contact with him. I just watched him, that was my plan, but we know how well they work out, right?

The same thing kept repeating in my head over and over that night as the soft music played, "Collin, I'm coming for you, I'm coming for you!" This was my own little foreshadowing into his bleak future, right? It made me sick to see all the women throwing themselves at him all night. What made him so special? Yes, he was very good looking and yes, very rich. He was tall with dark hair, great build, he wore that black tuxedo like it was cut just for him; he was a feast for the eyes.

I listened to him while he was on stage talking, talking all these people out of their money, money for the very people they pay no attention to out there, in their very own streets, but they could give a few bucks tonight to clear their conscience, right? Collin had that gift to empty their pockets for sure and I'm sure he used that same gift to get a few women to drop their panties as well. Then why kill them, what is it that makes Mr. Perfect kill? He could get or have anything or anyone he wanted, why kill then? I understand why I'm going to kill him, but why does someone like him kill?

After about four glasses of free Champagne, I began to make my way through the crowd of well-dressed rich people, again a feast for the eyes, dressed to the nines. They were all laughing and sipping Champagne while music played in the background. They had servers pushing around

Local Art from local painters on carts for everyone to bid on. I found myself just behind him, and I lightly brushed my body against his as I passed. I could feel myself beginning to get a sick feeling in my stomach. Then the feeling turned to pain, then to anger. At that moment, I knew I could handle this, like I handed the Romanian that night. This guy is a cold-blooded killer, Collin the killer. As I made my way past him, someone grabbed my arm; I turned to see it was Neal, one of my partners. "Shit" I didn't think this all the way through. He smiled and asked, "What are you doing here, Rae? We thought you were in Europe relaxing, after your tragedy?"

I looked right into his eyes and told him this was an important charity for me. I had to come and give to the lost women of my city. Reminding him that we helped to build this city, but no one was there for them, they have to live here, that they were here first, that no one thought of them when it came time to build those new shiny buildings.

I had always wanted to do a project for them on one of the outermost streets of the city. I said, "Rename the street, Sanctuary Street, a street with houses, shops and multilevel buildings for them to get a fresh start--- wouldn't that be something, Neal, something real... all inspired by the very women we are toasting here tonight. Neal, look up there, can you see yourself on that stage giving Sanctuary Street to the city - what a project to be proud of."

I watched Neal's face the whole time. I was spinning this story to him out of total crap; not really, I had this vision back in college, the innocent days of Raven Rousseau. And now I had him---hook, line and sinker... I guess I'm good at this stuff too. Neal felt like shit and Collin had better look out, here comes a new player in the streets of New Orleans, me! I'm coming for you, Collin....

To my surprise, Neal's wife Toni walked up with Collin---this was very uncomfortable. I didn't want this, it's too soon. I hadn't thought about how I would react being close, knowing what I knew. Toni grabbed my arm and pulled me close and said, "Collin, this is my one of my husband's partners at the firm, Raven Rousseau." He bowed and reached for my hand and said, "Very nice to meet such a beautiful woman and a partner in an all-male firm, very nice." I smiled and began to say thank you when he leaned forward and caressed my hand, as he kissed the top of it sending lightning like shocks all thought my body. Instantly giving me a crystal clear visions of women, lots of women, and their faces, their dead faces.

In that instant I saw them all, the women he had killed, so many. Neal spoke up, breaking the visions. He began telling Collin about me, and Collin never broke eye contact. I had his attention; I had a killer's attention. Collin had that look, that empty look some people have in their eyes, those empty soul-less black eyes---he had that dead look... I pulled away when Toni asked him to dance. I slipped behind a woman in a red satin dress and walked to the door as fast as I could without running, I didn't want to draw any attention, but running is what I wanted to do—run, and never stop.

I stepped outside the double doors and threw up on the red carpet that was stretched across the steps. I couldn't hold it in, he made me sick to my stomach, all those women's faces. I just doubled over and let go again. By this time a valet ran over to me yelling, "Ma'am, are you ok?

Let me help you to a cab." I waved him off and took off down the street into the night by myself, walking the empty streets and thinking---I was on his radar now. the next move was mine. What a head trip this was... Now what do I do next. First, I had to send Neal a text, thanking him for being there and that I was on my way to the airport to catch my flight back to Paris, and that I would be in touch with him soon, and to be thinking about the project I had proposed. That would get me out of that little mess up. Going forward I will have to be more careful.

Facing this horrible man is something I'm going to have to work on. I have to be able to be close to him or this will not work... I'll end up like the others, dead! To think about holding hands, or his face close to mine, his hands touching me, or having to kiss this guy just makes my skin crawl...

I know why I'm going to kill him, but that's different. He killed my sister. She was one of his little cheap toys, but now I know there are a lot of women out there he has done this to. I knew I had to be different. I'm not anybody's toy; he has to see me as a different type of woman. I know he has dated women without killing them; I did the research on him, through the Gazettes Society section. I looked up all the women he has been linked with and they are alive and kicking.

Where was one of those mind orgasms when I needed it. I would have thought him touching me and the visions would have put me over the edge like that night at the bar. The visions seemed to work out quite nicely for me. I had no fear, I took care of what I had to do, I never felt sick or scared, well maybe a little at first. So, I'm beginning to understand that it is the mind orgasms that change me, they put me in a hyper-alert state, a focused state, a fearless state. I believe Mary, my therapist, calls that a trigger; a switch in a person's brain that does something to the neurotransmitter things in your head or else she would say I'm delusional.

Ok then, I found my switch; I can use it to get my crazy on... that night at the bar I simply went into the bathroom and made myself have the visions, that is my trigger, my switch. Hey, Mighty Mouse changed in a phone booth, right...Ha-ha---it's nice to laugh for a change. After all, I'm just going after a man, to kill him, because he killed my sister, right?

I found myself walking downtown towards the business district of the Quarter as morning broke. I never went home, not sure why. I knew where I was and where I was heading. I was in a post mind orgasm determined mindset that was for sure. I stopped at the building of my new friend, Collin, the friend I met at the party last night. I stood outside his building with my hands pressed against the glass doors. Should I go in and find his office, do a little Nancy Drew on him, up close and personal? Mr. Real Estate guy, the rich one, the showman of the night, he must have raised thousands of dollars for that charity. A great charity for the lost women of New Orleans. I should make him build Sanctuary Street, after what he has done.

This guy has everything, why does he do such sick things? I guess I am learning the whys of this world, which Collin and the others walk every day, and there are others out there like him. This is a world that consumes their thoughts, their dark thoughts... Now someone is coming after *him* for a change.

I'm drifting a little off center myself, but it seems like a natural progression. I'm evolving, as Mary would point out. That is the big scary when you think about it. I have a mission of vengeance for my sister, so what is going to happen on the other side of this?

Jack, he is hunting this guy too. Should I just give him to Jack and be done with this and go back to my life as an architect in New Orleans and put this behind me? What is it that keeps me moving forward with this underworld of nastiness, killing, hurting, power, and sexual release? Our world is changing too. It is evolving into the playgrounds of evil and I'm one of its players now.

As I finally reached the apartment, something was off---like someone had been there, or something. I didn't notice the man across the street watching me from behind a tree as I got there. I went in and looked around, nothing looked to be out of place. I went right to the closet of Goth and changed into the outfit again, I figured I would be able to move around town without being recognized. I packed a few of her fun things to take with in case I needed to jump into a phone booth for a new look...

I was about to close the dining room entrance when a shadow crossed my face and I turned to see a man standing in the foyer---I grabbed a brass candle stick and held it out as I yelled, "who are you?" The man stepped into the dim light coming from the kitchen window. "No worries here lady, I'm a U.S. Marshal looking for Sara, do you know her? He said holding his badge up in front of him. I lowered the stick and told him, "I'm a friend of hers and I'm staying here for a couple of days."

He looked puzzled and asked when was the last time I saw her? I told him, it was about a week and a half ago, why? And why is the Marshal's office looking for her? He just looked at me and walked over to the sofa and sat. As I stepped closer, he said, "Are you the sister she was obsessed about finding?"

I just stopped and looked at him. Not knowing which way to go with this, I walked over to the settee and sat, not saying anything. He said Sara told me that she had a sister she never knew and had to find her.

"She would ask me to look into things for her from time to time, but it never went anywhere, damn Romanians. Did Sara find what she was looking for? Are you her sister?"

"What if I was, why are you in her life? What do you have to do with Sara? Who are these Romanians?"

"Ok, I will take a chance here, she is under protective custody as a material witness. This is a safe house."

I looked at him and said, "I call bullshit, Marshal, this is no safe house---maybe a playhouse---for all I know, you're just a toy she plays with and if she was under protective custody, she would be here now! You need to do better than that if we are going to continue this cat and mouse game or do you need me to strap you to the table in there, would that help you talk to me, Mr. Marshal?"

I could tell he didn't really know which way to take this now. I felt like making a run for the open door, but at the same time, I was curious as to why the Marshal's office was in my sister's life, or maybe this guy really was one of those guys that would play with her in the other room.

His phone rang, and he got up to answer it as he walked into the kitchen. I heard him say, "She's what---the FBI" At that point I quickly shot out the door and made my way down the stairs and ran to the alley that leads to the street behind the apartment. Luckily there was a cab sitting at the corner, I ran to it and jumped in, startling the driver. "Hey, sorry, let's go!"

He looked back to ask where, when I saw the Marshal run out of the front of Sara's place down the block---"just drive," I said. He took off. I had nowhere to go now, the FBI are watching my house, and the Marshals are at Sara's. I'm in a little bit of a pickle at the moment.

I needed a minute to think of the next move. I couldn't go to a hotel, they would ding my credit cards and know I'm still here. The Marshal had no real ID on me. Luckily I was still in this get-up. He wouldn't be able to tell Jack who I was or what I looked like, thank God! The only thing I could come up with was going home and sneaking in for a shower and fresh clothes. I had money and my passport in my safe and even more clothes at the airport locker. I had forgotten about that. Sara's bike is over there, on the side of my house. "Ok, what then, Ms. Super wannabe Killer, what's your next move?" No kidding around, this killer shit is very taxing on a person---no wonder most killers are crazy to begin with...

I knew I needed time to follow Collin and see how he operated, so I needed to put myself into his path. See just how a murderer lived life on a daily basis. This will be new, like I'm designing a building---same principle, right?

You start with the foundation and work up. Before I knew it, the cab had me at the street one over from mine. I didn't remember telling him where to go, I needed to sleep and rest my head---this killer shit is very taxing on the brain. I slipped out and made my way to the corner across from my house, there was a car out front watching it. I backtracked to the street behind my house and made my way through Ms. Charlotte's yard again. I waited to see if anyone was lurking around, nothing, so I made my way to the side door and went to turn off the alarm, but it wasn't on.

I looked around quietly to make sure no one was inside waiting, it looked clear and in I went. I stood in the kitchen holding the edge of the countertop amazed at what I had gotten myself into. Running from the FBI and the U.S. Marshals and the damn Romanian Gypsy Mob all in a week's time, you've got to give it to this girl---when I jump into a project, I do it in a big way... Oh, let's not forget, I'm going after a killer and I made a wonderful Haitian friend. Typical week for a girl like me, not! I made my way upstairs to the bathroom in the back part of the house to take a shower, with the lights off, not to alarm the guy's out front---I hope they don't take turns coming in and checking.

I finished my shower, feeling clean and a little bit normal now when I heard the front door open and the noise from a walkie-talkie. I stopped to listen, I heard the lid to the downstairs toilet hit the back of the tank. I just stood motionless in the hallway wrapped in a towel holding a bundle of clothes and a wig. I heard the toilet seat slap down and the sink turn on, well good--- they wash their hands. Next, I could hear someone walk around down there.

I started to panic, but then I heard the squeak of the front door. I made my way to the front bedroom and peeked out the window to see a man standing in my front yard lighting up a cigarette, then continuing to the car. I went to my bedroom and put some clothes on and filled a backpack with more. I then went back to the spare room and curled up on the floor next to the bed and window. It felt safer, I was out like a light.

Morning came and the car out front had changed---new guys now---I made my way down the back steps and was about to head out the side door, when, for some reason, I went into the living room, where I last saw Jack. I sat on the sofa when I noticed a speck of white paper in the cushions. I reached down and pulled on it, it was the flyer---did he see it, damn, what now...

Chapter 13

Mouse Trap

The clever cat eats cheese and breathes down rat holes with baited breath.
W.C. Fields

As the team made their way down to the Marina in Iberia Parish, D's laptop sounded, and everyone turned to see what just came in---Jack said, "Well, what do you have, sir...?"

"Nothing, I have nothing Jack. The guys at the lab are going to go over everything again but there is nothing, no prints, no other physical evidence, other than the sweat DNA," Domingo affirmed.

Jack sat quiet for about a second and then spoke up, "We operate as though we've got something on this guy---take no short cuts. I need eyes on everything a total 360 of this place - EJ, get us all the history and records you can find on the Marina."

"Jack, this isn't just a Marina, it's the fucking Port of Iberia. They call it the Gulf Coast Cajun Connection. The Port has total access to both interstate travel as well as open water travel---it builds and supplies offshore oil rigs and highway construction materials, and container shipping of course. That is just to start with. They have over a hundred companies and over 5000 employees. They do have a small area for personal boats and small ships, but Jack, they have 24/7 access for both, highway travel and open water---they must have local help---you know what that means. We can't trust anybody Jack..."

D spoke up, "Guys, I've pulled up a satellite map of the Port and area around it---not pretty, guys---there is only one feeder in and out of the Port by water, but the Port itself is spread out with four or five roads in or out. I see the small personal marina off South Lewis Street. Is that where we are looking for this guy?"

"Shit, hey EJ, pull into that diner on the left---we need some food and we can talk this out---the area is too large to just wander in and do our shit---we are running blind at the moment." EJ whipped into the parking lot to park and the team jumped out. Lizzy went in to find a table, the rest of the team filed in behind her. It's your typical roadside diner, with the long bar area overlooking the flat grill, and booths along the front, the team squeezed into the large round booth at the end near the restroom and kitchen doors. That was on purpose too, it had the best vantage point in the place---the team is in a hyper-alert state at the moment. They knew what they were after, but needed a plan.

The young waitress popped over to the table and filled them with that Deep South twang, "Hi there, what can I get y'all?"

The whole team shouted, "COFFEE PLEASE, we need coffee ma'am." She just laughed and ran behind the counter and grabbed the fresh pot and set it on the middle of the table. "I'll be back in a minute to get your orders, guys."

The team hit that pot of coffee like a raid on a drug house... They all set up their laptops and D loaded the satellite shot on the screen. They all were synced with his laptop for this and they started going over the possibilities.

Lizzy handed out files to everyone, which had every detail they had at this point, but not very much at all---D did a dual screen video thing with the lab in Baton Rouge. It was 'all hands on deck' for this operation, in case they could add anything.

The boys at the lab jumped right in with, "We found some dirt on the floor of the cabin that should not have been there. It was a type of sand used to do commercial sand blasting. We have narrowed it to the coast, somewhere that has offshore drilling materials because we also picked up matter only found on the sea floor just off the coast of Louisiana..."

"We kept digging and found a speck or two of blood on several pieces of the sand. We have typed at least three blood types so far---none matches your victim, sorry."

Jack looked over at Lizzy and asked, "Do you think we can get a warrant with that?"

Lizzy shook her head, then said, "Jack, only for the sand blasting shops out there, nothing else."

Jack shot back with, "What about the oil rig goop, that should cover it and get us on the property, so we can do the rest, the way we do our thing---you know, Lizzy."

"Jack, you know better. Everything we find would be thrown out and we would have nothing. We need something solid to keep our asses out of trouble this time---this is too big. Guys you know the second our vehicles hit the dirt out there, word will fly across the port, do we have anybody in there that we can trust or has been checked out and we can use?"

"I've been looking, there is a guy in the Port Authority that used to be on the N.O.P.D. Can you call Oliver and ask?" Jack jumped up and headed for the door while dialing Oliver's number on his phone.

"Hey bro, we need info on anyone that you may know out in Iberia Parish, The Port to be exact. Ollie, we need a guy on the inside to trust, or something we can use to control them, I don't care at this point---I just need an open ticket into the Port."

Oliver was quiet, and then spoke up with, "My auntie has a cousin out there, but I don't know too much about him. I'm pulling his jacket now---he is a Lieutenant on the job down there, but Jack, I don't hear good things about the guys out there if you know what I mean. I.A. has a special task force that watches the Port---anyway, I got his jacket, but one of his files is sealed? It will take me an hour at least with I.A. to get it unsealed for you, can I use your names with this as a peace offering to help get it unsealed?"

Jack told Ollie to do whatever he needed to.

"Bro, just call her and get your warrant, and stop the bull shit! She can get you that open ticket, call Dance." Jack started to twist and turn in the same spot he was standing, "She and I aren't on the best of terms at the moment."

Ollie just laughed and said, "Not showing up for your engagement dinner was a hard one to swallow, don't you think, and let's not forget she lobbed a bottle of champagne at your head the next morning when you told her you couldn't marry her. Hey, maybe she has forgotten all that, right...?"

Jack dropped his head, uncomfortable at the mere suggestion, "My guess, bro, is I'm screwed. Isn't there anyone one else we can go to?" asked Jack.

"Son, you have burned out just about everyone down here. That's why you moved, remember, buddy...?" Ollie said.

Lizzy flew out the door and grabbed Jack's arm, "Jack, give it a break; come and listen to what Domingo has," Lizzy said.

"Ok guys, I did a search on any type of unsolved ritual killings between here and New Orleans using what we have so far. Then I got thinking, this is an interstate case now, so I opened it to a nation-wide search and found a couple hundred unsolved cases that fit our victimology---and guys, they date back to the late eighties, yes, I said the late eighties," affirmed Domingo.

Jack spoke up with, "The fucking late eighties people, how the hell can we explain that? Christ, I know we will be able to filter some out due to geographical habits, but first, EJ, brief us on the most recent ones. Where they were found, what the body looked like at the scene. Let's start there so we can get a grid started. Then we can work it back to the eighties. And hope we don't need a bigger victim board to put all the photos on guys. This is crazy!"

"The victimology has to fit. That way, the number should drop, and we will know about how long this Display Killer has been doing this for sure... Let's look at this from the standpoint of the un-sub starting young, so take a look at those murders, they will be a little on the crude side, but still have all the similarities to the recent kills. Keep that in mind---he had to evolve into the patient, organized ritual display killer he is now."

"Jack, if this guy has been killing for this long and no one has put this together, what are our chances?" Furthermore, what is the ritual about? Is it the display? EJ asked.

"EJ, we started with a fresh kill this time, and we work the evidence, the DNA, the sand, the ocean muck---you know that, so let's bring it, girl--- Lizzy will work on the victimology and tell us a story."

Jack grabbed his phone and reluctantly called her, the woman he almost married. "Hey, Dance, it's Jack, how are you?" asked Jack with a hard swallow.

"Jack, my long-lost mistake, what do you want after all this time? I know you wouldn't have called me unless you needed something, you always need something, and nothing has changed about that, right Jack? By the way, MISTAKE, I already talked to Ollie---so cut the bullshit. I'm not going to stand in your way of an investigation, especially this one, the eighties, damn, Jack... I signed it twenty minutes ago, but thank you for calling yourself, that is big... and Jack, I hope you find the peace and happiness you need someday---good bye. Damn you, Jack, damn you..." Click.

Jack walked back inside. The teams were all standing ready, and Lizzy was holding a white piece of paper as Jack reached the table. Lizzy handed Jack the bill, the warrant, and her phone. Lizzy looked him in the eyes and told him, "It's Oliver." The team walked to the door and left Jack standing there holding Lizzy's phone.

"Hey, are you ok?" asked Scotty.

"Yeah, I'm good, I think---you could have let me know she signed off on the warrant bro..."

"Jack, I was busy running the paperwork through for you, just go get something we can work with. I called Bobby with the FBI Critical Response Team, local Swat and local back up also. They are meeting you just off interstate 83 were it meets Weeks Island Road. There is a big open lot on your right---you won't miss them."

"Ollie, can we trust these guys?" Jack asked.

"My gut tells me they have issues, but no one has been told what the operation is, not even Bobby, who we know we can trust. They all have instructions to just meet your team there for further instructions," replied Ollie.

"Thanks, I will have Domingo cover the radio chatter just in case." Jack looked back at D and told him, "The local Swat and our Critical Response Team along with local P.D. are waiting for us near the site---I'm pulling all cell phones when we get there and need you to track all chatter on all radio stations, ok? I mean across the board D, use your gizmos and get me something to go on..."

Lizzy smiled and said, "Making friends so soon, Jack? What are you going to tell these guys?"

Jack had that look on his face, the look that gets him and the team into trouble most of the time. But he knew he couldn't back down---shit was happening at the Port, and they couldn't risk losing this guy, John Gardner, and any information he might have.

Their black SUV rolled into the lot and took the front position. The team jumped out and went to the rear of the vehicle and suited up before talking to anyone. The two team leaders walked over and introduced themselves, Bobby from CRT and Lieutenant Colter from local Swat.

Bobby began to ask what the operation was, when Jack cut him short and told them, "This is a high priority operation. I need all your men and the local officers as well, in one group for the brief. We need to be on the same page, plus we will answer all your questions and get this underway, gentlemen." They all headed towards the group with Jack and his team fanning out to both sides.

"Hey everyone, I'm Jack Bode' with the FBI and this is my team. Sorry for the short notice and mystery. This op is of high priority and needs to be handled as such---there will be NO, I repeat NO, outside communication We will need all your cell phones---no exceptions, this will be a radio only operation. We are hitting the Port hard, and I need local to block off all roads in or out. We have the Coastguard in position in the river now. They will handle all water and air activity. My team is handing out a picture of who we are looking for, but keep your eyes open for anything."

Jack's team began watching and reading all their faces to see if they could see anyone who had a problem with the order, while they watched the Swat and CRT team leaders gather the phones.

The team leaders walked them over to Domingo and handed him all the phones. Domingo took the phones and walked over to their SUV. Jack looked at Lizzy and told her to ask the team leaders for their phones also. "Gentlemen, no exceptions--this is too important, thank you."

Lizzy held out her hand and the CRT leader handed his over with no problem, but the Swat leader Lieutenant Colter became upset, explaining he had to stay in touch with his boss, and that his command has never been questioned.

Jack and the team all walked over to him, and began asking what the issue was--why would it matter? What's up? Telling him, he could use his radio, headquarters would be monitoring the chatter.

Jack gave him a Jack smile and said "Lieutenant, you will be with me for the operation. Swat will be with EJ and CRT will be with Lizzy. CRT leader Bobby and two local officers will take Port Authority and shut down all communications in or out. I do suggest you get their cell phones also... "This man we are looking for, is wanted in connection with a murder in Ascension Parish. He has two ID's---one is Romanian and has been deported once already---the other is an American, John Gardner from New Orleans."

Mumbling filled the crowd and stopped Jack cold.

"You got something on this gentleman? Please speak up, now", Jack ordered. The local officers were huddled, talking. Jack walked over with D right behind him, and busted in the huddle and asked, "What do you know, gentlemen, lay it out now. We are wasting time! Now is the time to share, and to do it fast!" They all looked at each other and began telling Jack that John Gardner was the owner of one of the offshore oil rig construction companies. That everyone knew him around here. Jack asked them why Port Authorities or Immigration wouldn't have said anything. He should have popped up on both their lists.

They had no idea why, and explained that they never really got any calls from the Port. It seemed clean, and was handled from within. Except for a call about a year ago, about a body floating near Marsh Island, but that's not near the Port. Jack looked at D, he was already hitting the keys to his laptop. "Jack, female and thirteen years old, a European girl, did I say thirteen? Jack I'm sending Lizzy the file now." Jack thanked the officers and walked over to Lizzy and asked if there were any photos of the body. Lizzy pulled up the images and showed Jack.

"What are you looking for?" she asked.

"Ligature marks, marks on the body! Something we can tie together. Can you get these photos to Baton Rouge fast? Over and above that, have them look specifically for body marks of any kind, cuts, burns, strap marks, ligature marks and get back to us ASAP!"

Lizzy ran back to the truck and finished up with the file. Jack walked over to D and the men. D pointed the screen at Jack, and then placed his finger on a name, the name of the investigator who handled the case a year ago. It was Lieutenant Colter. Jack looked up and didn't see him in the group and asked where he was---one of the men said he walked over to the building to piss...

Jack took off running for the building with EJ on his tail. As they were about to open the door, a screaming black unmarked car came flying into the lot with lights flashing.

It was Oliver. Ollie kicked the car door open and ran over to Jack and whispered, "It's him, Colter is the leak", in Jack's ear. They all pulled their weapons and charged the building, followed by every officer on site, they had it surrounded within a couple of seconds while Jack, Ollie and EJ burst inside and had their weapons pointed at the Lieutenant as he stood behind the store counter holding a cell phone in his hand.

Oliver rushed him and pinned him to the desk. He told Jack that I.A. was looking at him for a number of things including being involved with the Romanian Mob---if not being one of its leaders, his last name is Romanian and it means BOSS. He has family back in Romania. Lizzy grabbed the phone and tossed it to Domingo.

Chapter 14

Gypsy Queen

It is the dim haze of mystery that adds enchantment to pursuit.

Antoine Rivarol

Wait, this works perfectly for me, it gives me time, I like time, I need time to find Collin, to play with Collin, to learn more about Collin the killer. Jack would've been all over Collin and I wouldn't be able to move on him or the plan. So, I will take this as a win for team Raven. I slipped out the side door and was gone again. I had to call in a favor though. Jean-Paul would have to help me now.

I made my way back to the market we were at last night. I looked through the window to see if Maximus was working, I saw him come out of the back and examine the food cases. So, I went in and stood at the case, called his name. He looked at me with a puzzled look on his face. I smiled then told him that I was the lady from last night with Jean-Paul, and I needed to get hold of him.

He smiled and pulled out his cell phone, dialed a number and handed it to me. Maximus remarked that I looked different today. I heard someone speaking in Haitian on the other end, I said, "Jean-Paul, it's Raven, can you meet me here at the market? He didn't hesitate and told me to stay inside the market---he would explain when he got there. He asked me to hand the phone back to Max, demanding again not to move or go near any windows.

I saw a single chair next to the food cases and sat there bent over with my head in my hands and suitcases at my feet. When Maximus asked if I was hungry, I told him I was starving. He smiled and disappeared behind the food case for a minute or two then emerged with a sandwich and coffee. I looked up at him and said thank you for everything. He just smiled and took me by the hand, gently pulling me to the back room, telling me in very broken English that I needed to stay out of sight for now.

It seemed like it took Jean-Paul forever to get there. I was getting a little restless, so I moved to the edge of the backroom doorway to look around the corner into the deli area. There I could see the front door. I saw a man sitting in a car across the street watching, and another car parked just outside the market. It looked like Jean-Paul, but I couldn't be sure.

Maximus came over to me and said, "Follow me---you can't go out the front---they are waiting for you."

I said, "Who is waiting?"

"The Romanians. They tracked you both here from the other night---there is a word out on the street to find you and return you to them in any condition." Jean-Paul is going to meet you down the way at the corner. I will show you the way." Maximus took me through a door that led to the empty building next to the market and then to another, then another until we reached the end of the block at Barracks Street.

Jean-Paul was standing next to the side door of the building and motioned for me to come out. He grabbed me and shuffled me into the backseat of the car. I had never seen this car. He told me to lay down and cover myself with the blanket on the floor for now. He hugged his brother, and got in. He took a minute to looked around, then sped off heading north on Barracks Street.

I freaked out and asked what was going on? He just motioned with his hand to stay down. He began explaining that the guys from the other night at the club were able to track us to the deli and have been watching it ever since.

"You made an impression on the Boss, and now he wants you, and will probably kill you for disrespecting him in front of his people---or he may just want to play with you. I'm not going to let you find out which. We must make you disappear for a while and let him cool off. Where do you want to go?"

I slid up a little and popped my head out, just my eyes and nose though. I never told Jean-Paul what I was really up to---fully anyway. I didn't know if he would understand, or turn me in---he does have a couple of choices now, Mob or FBI... I explained what had happened with the Marshal, and when Jan-Paul finally stopped laughing, I told him I was in a pickle! He turned and looked at me and asked, "What is a pickle, I don't know this?"

It was my turn to laugh and it felt good for a minute. I explained that it meant I had nowhere to go and had not thought this all the way through.

He told me it was a good thing I had changed, changed into normal woman clothes. They only know you as the white haired lady, the lady that made the boss grovel like a little baby. He looked back at me again and said it quite seriously.

"You could take the organization right out of his hands now if you wanted it and be the Gypsy Queen of New Orleans. I would help and be right by your side!" Jean-Paul had that look in his eyes that was the same look I had that day at Sara's when I looked at myself in the mirror. I sat quietly for a minute thinking about what he had just said. Me, Raven, the head of the New Orleans underworld... What a thought... right?

Jean-Paul told me about a place in Biloxi, Mississippi just an hour and a half from here. They have nice places to stay and lots of people to hide with. Biloxi is one of those places people go to hide, forget, and be someone they are not---the place can make you in a minute or break you forever. Lower than when you got here, however, no white hair this time! I told him I liked the idea, but to take me to the airport first, that I needed to get something.

He nodded. I smiled and we both sat back quietly, not saying anything else for the rest of the trip. I looked out my window and watched those damn wooden power poles flip by like I did as a child. Those poles were my way of dealing with, forgetting, dreaming of better times, times my dreams had me playing a different role in life, not one of being a killer looking for a killer or being the Queen of the underworld. Adulthood, what a real bitch, right...?

Watching the poles on this trip, I was not flashing back, I was flashing forward. This was different for me. Like that whole building a building from scratch thing. The architectural thing I've studied and used with every project. My mind was beginning to plan the hunt, the hunt for Collin and the foreplay I will use to bait the killer and draw him in. And not get myself killed in the process, of course.

Just listen to my bad self now---I'm, well I am a little Cray--Cray, but I believe, once he sees that a woman can stand toe to toe with him and play hard like he does, he might respect that. I still need to find out why he does this and how many he has killed. What is he hiding behind; what pushes him do this. What the hell am I talking about---I'm just going to kill the bastard and go home to my normal life again! What is normal, again? It seems to get blurry very easily now.

We made it to the airport arrivals area. I asked Jean-Paul if he would go in and go to locker #124 and bring me the bag that was in there. He reached back for the key, then went on his way without saying a word.

 About five minutes later he returned and handed me the bag, and off we drove on our way to Biloxi.

I just stopped thinking and watched the poles flip by again and must have fallen asleep. The trip to Biloxi was only an hour and twenty from the French Quarter, I did like the trip over Lake Pontchartrain, then watching the coast line on the way up, but I was out, hopefully dreaming of good stuff.

The next thing I remembered was Jean-Paul asking me which Hotel did I like? I popped up and said I had no idea, I had never stayed here before, just drove through. He spoke up and said. "My manman, works at Harrah's Gulf Coast Hotel and Casino, would that work?"

I sat up straight, and had to ask, "Your Manman?"

"Sorry, that's mother in Haitian Creole," He said with a smile. I told him that would be perfect, not knowing that this single trip would start a new wave of life for me. I do mean a wave... Jean-Paul pulled up to the door and opened my door for me. He then walked to the trunk and pulled my two suitcases out and stood beside me.

The Valet from the hotel walked over and Jean-Paul spoke to him in Haitian. The Valet nodded and ran over to the outside desk, made a call, then waved to Jean-Paul.

 I looked at Jean-Paul with a puzzled look on my face and he looked down at me and whispered, "Just follow my lead and everything will be fine. You will be taken care of, I have taken care of everything."

I just stood there and waited, when two more Valets came out from the hotel and shook Jean-Paul's hand. They were all speaking Haitian Creole. One took my suitcases and the other led me into the hotel. As we walked up to the front desk, I watched Jan-Paul who was standing behind a pillar and a plant, not wanting to be seen, but making sure I was ok. Then I saw a woman dressed in a chef's jacket come up behind him and grab his arm, then hugged him. That must be his mother, a smaller woman than I had thought. He looked over at me and smiled.

I turned back to my two Valets. They were talking to this absolutely beautiful Haitian woman behind the check-in desk who reached out and took my hand in hers, then smiled reassuring me of no worries. "You are in good hands," then whispered, "Do not trust the hotel staff, just us, and you will be safe." She handed me a room key and off we went to the elevators. I didn't see Jean-Paul after that. We walked down a long hall, and at the end was a window that looked out onto the waters of the Gulf. I enjoyed the view while waiting on the elevator. I noticed we used the service elevator, a little strange but I went with it.

We landed on the ninth floor and headed down the hall to its end. I heard a door pop to my right, and they led me in to this beautiful suite that had a full view of the gulf from large open windows across the entire front of the room and three sets of full floor to ceiling glass sliding doors that opened onto a balcony. I was in a dream at this point.

The two men had unpacked my clothes, plus one popped the cork on a bottle of champagne, while the other placed my special case on the desk next to the window. Talk about spoiling a girl. They told me if I needed anything, to call the numbers written on a paper, a piece of the hotel stationary. They then handed me a small flip phone. "Please do not call the desk, Call these numbers for safety, and only use this phone please. Jean-Paul has set this up for you. You will be very safe and treated like a Queen, per his instructions." I was overwhelmed by all this. They smiled and let themselves out.

I walked around the suite for a minute enjoying the view. I even stepped out on the balcony and the wind took my hair. I could feel it push against me. That feeling of its power was something else. I couldn't help but have this knowingness of power myself.

I wandered back in and found the master suite, walked to the king-sized bed---and flopped on the bed face down. The last thing I remembered was taking a deep breath---out like a light. I needed the rest, or I should be honest and say my head needed the rest. So much going on, being hunted and hunting myself, being new to this lifestyle, a hunter's life style, a killer's lifestyle. At least I can bring a little class to it, right...?

I woke about two hours later and knew the first thing I had to do was call Neal, to cover my tracks. He picked up right away, "Neal, I wanted to check in and see how things were going?" Neal was a little slow to respond. It was after ten and he must have been asleep. "Hey Rea, we were sleeping, but it's ok. Toni says hi and hurry home, she misses you. Nevertheless, what's going on with you---are you coming home soon?"

I explained that things started to get better when last night I ran into four nice people that knew Sara and we spent the evening looking at pictures of her time in Paris. I told him how it pulled me down again and by the end of the evening I was feeling bad again. I think I'm going to leave Paris and travel down to Italy and try to forget again. I miss my work, especially here, being around all the French and Italian Grand architecture.

Neal began to explain that a lawyer stopped by and left an envelope for me. Neal said he put it in my top drawer for when I returned. I thanked him and asked if anyone else had been by asking any questions? He told me "no", not since those two detectives or FBI people were here in the beginning. I told Neal how much I appreciated his understanding and help. That we will have to go to dinner at Domenica at the Roosevelt when I get home. I knew it was Toni's favorite in town.

I told Neal that if a man stopped by, by the name Jean-Paul---please give him the envelope and only him. Please be discreet with this for me, reporters and all. That it was very important. He understood and told me not to worry.

Just before we hung up I said, "and Neal, please take the envelope and put it in your safe just in case and to make sure to start the new project we talked about (Sanctuary Street)." He just laughed, and then told me the board had already approved it and we have been scouting areas and properties. For some reason, Neal was easy to manipulate, at least for me...that is. "I guess that is what a real friend is, right? Maybe I will give Mary my Therapist a call and ask her what she thinks about this---friend, or a manipulative pawn to play with thing? And do I really know the difference myself?

Chapter 15

The Port, The Leak and Mr. Gardner

'The battle-line between good and evil runs through the heart of every man.'

Aleksandr Solzhenitsyn

"We have to hit the Port NOW, move, everyone is on go... Shut it down and find me this guy. Alive please! D, did he make a call from that cell?"

D focused on his laptop, hitting the keys, as the SUV rocked from side-to-side, then yelled up to Jack, "Jack, he made two calls, one to the Port area and the other to New Orleans proper. If I got this right, it was to a cell in the Port Authority office, and Jack, the phone is active now!

"No D, I need to know if you got this right?", bantered Jack.

"The number is 337-243-0099, Jack. You heard me, right?"

"No, he didn't hear you, but I did!", barked Lizzy from the front seat of the SUV as they sped to the Port. Jack was next to her listening to the other team's movements and didn't hear Domingo. D was working frantically on the other number, when they stopped in front of Bayou Rigs Inc.

Jack hit the ground running and headed for the door with the Swat team and Lizzy following close behind. The Swat team broke off into two units and began filtering around the building. Jack, called out on his radio, "Put the choppers in the air now, close down all water traffic and watch for anything going up river also. Do you copy?"

A click sounded, and a voice rang out, "We are a go for air and water shut down. We are hot for infrared cameras, they are up, we are in the air---copy---this is Chopper 1---we have activity on the south end of the Port right now, I repeat, you have two small boats entering the water and heading into the grass, we are in pursuit and the water craft teams are ready, they ain't going anywhere brother... Copy that!"

On the other side of the Port, Jack hit the door of the office with Lizzy at his back. He swung left, she swung right, but there wasn't anyone anywhere, nothing or nobody---a Swat officer was looking back at Jack from an open door at the rear of the office, he gave Jack the 'all clear'. This was a shadow office for sure. Jack and Lizzy ran back to the truck, while Jack was getting reports second by second on his headset from all the teams on the ground.

P.D. reported they had stopped two semi-trucks on a back road with two undocumented men driving them. EJ and CRT clicked in that they were holding four containers along with nine gunmen pinned down in one of the open containers. The men were unidentified at the moment. The choppers were pushing the two small boats right into the hands of the Coast Guard Special Teams Unit, ready in air boats set up in the grass across from the Port.

Bobby let Jack know that they had control of the Port Authority office. He said, "No calls going out Jack, and we are watching the monitors for anything moving."

Jack was happy and said, "We are off to a good start, gentlemen," which rang out over the radio.

"Jack, we have the Port Office, but---does anyone have eyes on Immigration? Jack, I'm concerned, they are not active on the radio, we've got nothing," said Bobby.

Jack looked at Lizzy and told her to get Swat over there and check it out. She looked over at him with a "Roger that, Boss," as Jack and Domingo jumped out near the Port office. Lizzy along with the Swat units, headed to the immigration office to check on their situation.

Jack and D were about to enter the office when Lizzy broke in with, "immigration looks empty, Jack---they cleared out fast, it seems."

After hearing that, Jack called out to EJ to check those gunmen at the containers for ID, and report back if they are our missing Immigration Officers.

Coming in on the main road to the Port were more local Officers and FBI agents arriving for back up. At this point, Jack called out for a total report on all activity.

"Teams, with local P.D. and more of our agents showing up on scene now, we know that word has to be out to the press by now, so be on the lookout, and keep them out---keep a blanket on the Port...!" asserted Jack.

The Coast Guard called back with, "We've got your guy, and another boat full of cash and two women, where do you want them?"

Local P.D. jumped in with, "We've got the two trucks headed out on the north side, Jack. They are filled with guns and drugs big time, where do you want these guys?"

EJ and CRT shouted out with, "Jack, we have a container full of women and children mostly female and another one with, well---everything needed for an over water get-a-way. It's filled with food, water, wine---good wine, money in different currencies, two cars, gold, drugs - coke, X, and heroine. The front is set up like an apartment, yes, an apartment, with state of the art satellite hookups."

"But Jack, we also have a case, a brief case with documents---ID's---very good ones, passports, social security cards, credit cards---these had cost big money, unquestionably professional and a ledger. Jack---Jack, we have their books---we have a handwritten ledger, Jack. This is on the whole freaking Port operation and something called Masquerade. We are on our way to your location now, EJ out."

Lizzy told all the other teams to bring everything to Port Authority. "We will set up there. We need local to keep all access roads closed to all traffic out or in, plus keep an eye on any in-coming vehicles that may look suspicious. Under no circumstances let any press in here, or near here. I mean no press until we are ready! I want them camped off the Port. Actually---position them in the lot off 86, where we set up this morning---that parking lot---Hey, local, you need to make that happen."

"All choppers need to keep eyes open for any after-activity, and remember to shut out any press choppers---boys, I mean shut them out! The whole purpose of us using radios was to eliminate outside traffic."

Jack and Domingo entered the Port office and headed over to Bobby, noticing everyone was on their knees, zip tied. Bobby had the Port comptroller in his office waiting on Jack and Lizzy.

Within minutes, Jack's team had arrived and started setting up the offices into a control center with two rooms for interrogation using CRT as in-house security, for obvious reasons. About that time, more local P.D. Chiefs rolled in and other FBI supervisors were filing in from other field offices for back up.

Those Police Department Unit Chiefs were not so happy looking though, having no idea what the FBI was doing shutting down a Port---an International Port---in their city. Jack, Bobby and Lizzy were at one of the desks talking, while all the Unit Chiefs argued amongst themselves.

Domingo had taken control of the terminal computers and was already running checks on all their systems.

Jack asked what EJ had turned up with the gunmen and containers. Lizzy said the guys were the immigration officers and they were insisting they found the containers, but the funny thing is, two of the men had the keys and codes to open the container's inner compartment; one guy had a Cuban cigar in his shirt pocket. It's not looking good for them at this point. There was no radio chatter or calls for back up. Jack told her they were to be treated as hostiles. Lizzy radioed EJ with Jack's orders, then made sure all the other radio channels were shut down except for EJ's, for Jack's brief. Domingo had all the other radio chatter running through his ear piece, just in case something went upside down on the ground.

Jack began to break down the plan, step by step---"First, I want the cell phones placed in front of their owners. I want the Lieutenant, cuffed, in a chair right in front of the interrogation room. Gardner would see we have the inside guy." Jack looked over at Domingo and asked, "Do you have that other number yet? Please say yes..."

Domingo walked over to Jack and showed him the screen and pointed to the number and the name of the person---then whispered that "it's active and it's here in the room now!" Jack turned and gave Lizzy a look that would bend steel. Lizzy moved toward Jack.

Jack turned and called out to Captain Pitchley, from the Criminal Interdiction Unit, one of the Chief's. "Captain Pitchley, can you help us with a little something? It's not the usual, we know, sir, but it will give us the upper hand. Let me lay it out for you, sir. We have the top-ranking members of a smuggling operation here at the Port. They are on their way here now, and I need to show them we have a high-ranking officer in custody, to get them to talk, can we use you as a decoy for the operation?" Jack conveyed.

"What do you need me to do, agent?" asked the Captain.

"Sir, all we need for you to do is sit in this chair next to the Lieutenant, like we have you in custody, that's all," quipped Jack, holding back a smile, a smile with a touch of mockery.... All eyes in the room were on Jack and the Captain. At this point it would be suspicious for the Captain to refuse. Jack cuffed only one of his hands to the chair and removed the Captain's gun from its holster.

Jack didn't want to tip him off yet, that they knew he was one of the Romanian Leaders working on the inside.

Lizzy was standing in the doorway by this time, watching Jack like he had lost his mind, when Jack motioned for her to go over to Domingo. Lizzy walked over to him, as he pointed to one of the screens and Lizzy's head jerked up and she looked over at Jack. Jack was asking the Captain if the cuffs were too tight at that time, and the Captain just shook his head, 'no'. Jack looked at the two and smiled a smile of satisfaction...

Jack patted the Captain on the shoulder and said thank you, then he made his way to the others across the room to brief them on what was about to happen; Lizzy, Bobby, Domingo, and the remaining Unit Chiefs gathered at the other side of the room out of ear shot. Jack got right to it and finished the brief for the plan.

 "Again, Domingo will call both numbers, and then we will see who wins the prize here at the Port. I want Lizzy standing next to the Captain as his cell rings, she will grab it, and that will be conformation he is one of our guys."

"When the other cell rings, that person will be forcibly put in another room for questioning. Keep them all separated from one another, with the blinds open for all to see. Most important is that all the players see we have taken down the Lieutenant and have the Captain as well, the two guys on the inside. Thanks to Domingo and his magic fingers, by the way. This is how we will get somewhere with these guys. Three rooms, Lizzy in one, EJ has another and Bobby and I will work the third, Gardner... We will switch every thirty minutes and compare statements."

Lizzy asked, "Who will break first? My money is on the Lieutenant. And Jack, we have an ETA on when Justice will be here! FYI Jack, I sent a chopper to get them about twenty minutes ago, it should be on the ground shortly," affirmed Lizzy.

"Have we worked with them? Or are they new to us?" Jack asked. Jack explained he was concerned with any outside players, and with trusting them. No one jumped in with an answer---so Jack radioed the chopper and told them they needed fuel and do a maintenance check, do they copy?

"Roger that, Jack, it's your ass man, but we've got you."

Lizzy looked at Jack and asked. "How is all this shit related to Sara's murder, or are we in some total other shit now, Jack---I don't want to lose focus on what we started here, do you?"

Jack stood at the window and said nothing. He knew things were a little crazy at the moment, but he really didn't have an answer for Lizzy.

"Jack, you know that Justice is coming to shut you down?" Bobby asked. He had been through this many times before, with not only Jack, but other teams that walked a little on the wild side---just a little.

"That's why we will have statements from all involved for them to chew on by the time they get here. We will give Justice all the credit for operation, and they will have to be happy with it, because, when they step off the chopper, they will see a reporter standing there giving a report on the Port situation.

I need someone to find a reporter in this area we know and trust. That's a funny statement about a press person, right?"

"So, I need a reporter, and have them on the air as the Department of Justice and I.A. touch down. They won't have any choice, but to smile and take it... Our fun starts in ten minutes, people---get ready."

Chapter 16

Anonymous...

'On wrongs swift vengeance waits!'

Alexandr Pope

My doorbell rang at 7am, followed by a knock. I staggered to the peephole and saw that it was a female in a hotel uniform, I opened the door while she stood there with a tray of coffee, orange juice, a water bottle and two small steaming towels, that smelled of jasmine. I had a puzzled look on my face when she introduced herself,

"Hello, I'm Hialeah, I'm with the spa---it's time for your morning massage and hair time" She said with a smile "Just throw on your hotel robe and slippers---lets go."

"Ok, sounds so great. I will be back in a second," Boy, they weren't kidding about the treatment here, for sure. Talk about spoiling a girl... We took the service elevator again, this time to the sixth floor and the spa was right there as the doors opened. The spa overlooked the Gulf. She walked me into a small room and opened the sliding doors to let the sound of the waves in. I felt a rush of goosebumps take over my body. She asked me to lay face down on the table. Of course, I didn't hear her as I was lost in the sounds of the waves from the Gulf in the distance. I could smell vanilla throughout the room---I love that smell---Sara's smell.

I began to drift, but not too far before I laid myself on the table to take it all in, the anonymous pampering I mean. I was there for at least two hours. Then after my hair was done they walked me to a cushy lounge chair, as other women walked in holding bathing suits for me to try on.

Heck, at this point I just went with it all---but not letting my guard down, well, maybe just a little---it would be very easy to forget who I am and what I was about to do. I changed into the bright orange tiny bikini and I knew I didn't need to be attracting attention, but I was feeling good today.

The girls took me down to the pool and set me up in a cabana across from the pool bar and bathrooms. I could see everything. Behind me was a full back drop of tropical trees and foliage for a safety cover and privacy---nice touch.

I sat on the edge of the lounge chair as they set everything up---food tray with all healthy stuff, fruit, juice, yogurt---I asked if I could get a poached egg and toast, the attendant pulled out a radio and made the call. She gave me a smile and a nod. The TV was set to a local news channel, and my chair was set for a perfect view of the pool and the other guests having fun.

I just took in all the scenery and sipped on my coffee and nibbled on some fruit, waiting for my eggs. I had no worries in the world. My mind was working overtime, though. I mean this whole set up, I could be as anonymous as I needed to be here, anywhere for that matter---anonymous is who I needed to be, the new me. I think I found out how to do that... and feel great doing it, right!

My new life just took a turn, a very nice turn. Anonymous me...This feeling was short lived though, the news cast was reporting on the events happening at the Port of Iberia back home and they mentioned Jack and the FBI. That had my instant attention. The Port, why was Jack down there, and not in New Orleans? Why weren't they looking for Sara's killer? How did the Port fit in with all this?

A very loud screaming man from India who sat across the pool, next to the slide, broke my attention from Jack and the news. I watched the man dressed in gold---I mean around his neck, fingers and wrists, even his teeth---to top it off he was wearing a French cut bathing-suit, not a good sight. His loud mouth, was drawing attention to himself. He was acting like a two year old. He made sure the whole pool area saw him.

He had two beautiful children, who were sitting next to an absolutely beautiful Indian woman that would just stop traffic in any country. She looked scared, visibly scared of him. They were also in a cabana like mine, but that didn't help his loud mouth---everyone would glance over, but no one would get involved. Now, here I was focused on the asshole, like a wildcat on her prey. Flashes of Sara hanging in that tree didn't help---I had a brief shiver that ran like a ghostly touch over my skin. I couldn't hear or understand what he was droning on about...so, I walked over to the pool's edge, and still couldn't understand. So, I took a quick dip in the pool to focus. By the time I surfaced, he had stopped and sat down. So, I went back to my cabana and watched some more news about the FBI and the Port, they were trying to ask Jack about the raid. All I could see were those blue eyes that boy had. Jack, what an intense hottie he is...!

Ok, I got up and walked down to the edge of the deck area and watched the Gulf waves roll in with the sun in full force. I closed my eyes and lifted my face to the sun while I listened to the waves for a minute, nice...

I was headed back to my cabana when I heard a "Hello". I turned to see who just said hello. The cabana was closed, when from across the pool the yelling started again and took my attention, well everyone's, for that matter. I turned to see what was happening and saw that it was the Indian family. I had forgotten the "Hello" from behind and headed to my cabana. No sooner did I sit down than the yelling, all in Indian, got heated. I saw what was about to be a problem, in his body language.

"Shit", he couldn't have waited until I left? He had to go and slap his wife as she cowered on the floor of the cabana. He grabbed one of the kids by the arm and threw both of his kids in the pool. What a dirt bag this guy was!

I called my attendant over and asked her, "What is his deal?"

She looked at me and shook her head, and said, "I can't."

I tilted my head back at her and asked her to please tell me.

"Ma'am, he is bad news. His name is Karl Agarwal, and he owns two or three of those cheap shopping center gambling places, where he cheats the old people out of their money. He never stays here at the hotel---he's too cheap, he just uses the pool area to show off. None of the staff likes him, he is rude and never tips, and we have never heard his poor wife, or the kids, speak a word."

Raven looked at her and asked, "Then why does the management let them back in? Just throw them out!"

The attendant smiled and said, "Well, they tried that, but he called corporate and fed them an ear full, and now it's like no one can touch him."

"Really," said Raven, "We will have to see about that! Can you hand me that case please, and shut the flaps for me as you step outside... Sorry, I'm not mad at you. By the way, what is your name?"

The attendant turned and said, "Daphne---that is my name, ma'am," as the girl smiled back at me.

"Well, Daphne, I have some work to do. You're my girl now, and I am going to be a couple of minutes, so don't leave or let anyone in, ok?"

"Yes, ma'am."

"Daphne, it's time to deal with that man properly, so you may want to call Jean-Paul and tell him I may need a ride and rescue soon!"

I watched Daphne's face change, to a darkened distressed look, as if she were afraid of his name.

"Yes, ma'am, I will have him called for you."

"Daphne, are you ok? You look scared, why?"

She looked down and shook her head, no! I stood and put my hand on her shoulder and asked her to talk to me, reassuring her everything was ok.

She looked into my eyes and said, "He is a very important man from where we are from." I motioned for her to sit with me and talk. She looked around like her life depended on it, and she was definitely scared... She took a breath and began telling me about who Jean-Paul really was, back home in their country. "He was above all the military Generals, and only answered to the President, until the overthrow," she said. "Things got bad and many tried to leave, but a lot of them were quietly killed."

By the time she and her family got here, he had already set up the 'Faksyon' or Faction in English, was what she called it. They answered to them---they got them jobs and places to live, along with protection.

"We pay them a little, and we answer to them for whatever they need."

I asked her if they were just in New Orleans and Mississippi, and she told me that the Faksyon was in what we call the Deep South, but she didn't understand what that was.

I explained what that meant, and she began telling me that I was an important person to them and I was to be taken care of at all costs. That anything I needed was to be done for me, which came from Jean-Paul himself. I was a little taken aback by that, but got a nice feeling at the same time---thinking this will be useful for my project and in the near future.

"By the way Daphne, I tip very well," and handed her a hundred-dollar bill! "Put that in your pocket, not theirs, understand?" She smiled and said she understood.

As Daphne stepped out I opened the case and pulled out a beautiful red wig, not an outrageous red, a nice red. I slipped it on and threw a towel around my midsection as a wrap to cover my suit, but leaving my legs and a little ass hanging there, just to make sure the attention was given! I popped on my sunglasses and headed out the back panel of the cabana and headed towards the pool bar. Karl was headed there as well. After the scene he had just made, I guess he needed a drink and some air...

I had made it to the bar seconds before him and asked the bartender for a Bloody Goose, when Karl started in... "Pretty lady, don't you know how to order a proper drink? You need a man to do that for you!"

This guy wasted no time in making advances and offending me in the process, wait---I did forget that women are not considered important where he is from.

I turned with a smile and began to walk over to him, he was standing at the end of the bar that faced the bathrooms. This sad little man couldn't help himself, looking me up and down and never really making it to my eyes---this guy was a piece of some bad work, really bad. I put my finger on his forehead, he was only five feett two to beat all. I pushed his head back and looked down into his eyes then asked if that worked with all the women?

Before he had a chance to answer, I had taken off my left high heel and jammed the heel spike into his throat---watching his eyes roll back, then kneed him in his special place and shoved him back towards the bathrooms, it only took a couple of pushes, but he made it, no one seemed to notice, but who would really care, right? On the door of the women's bathroom was a 'closed for cleaning' sign. That works for me, in we went, and bumped right into the girl cleaning it.

She just smiled and said, "Get what you give, that karma shit...," as she spit at the man then walked out and shut the door behind her.

By this time, he was on his hands and knees gasping for air. I walked around him, circling him several times, and then landed the point of my shoe in his ass crack sending him face first to the wet and sandy bathroom room floor. Karl was just moaning in pain.

"Karl, can you hear me?" I heard nothing but moans, so I knelt at his head and repeated myself, "Karl, can you hear me? I don't like how you treat your wife and kids or people in general, do you hear me?---you really need to hear me Karl! Tell me you hear me Karl!" Karl's squeaky moans filled the empty bathroom. I grabbed my high heel again, and then took his black greasy hair in my hand, lifting his head while holding the point of my spiked heel at his right eye and asked if he heard what I had said. I could feel him trying to nod against my grip...

I began telling him, "You are going to be kind to everyone you meet from now on, a Saint of a man, aren't you Karl?" He tried to nod again. I pushed the point of the heel closer to his eye and told himthat, "If I saw or was told by any of my people, that you have been a bad boy, all your cheap little gambling stores will burn to the ground and I will personally come for you. Karl, touch your wife or kids again and you will feel more than my heel in your eye, you had better remember this day or I will return for vengeance. Do you know what that means?"

He just gagged with bubbles of drool falling from his mouth.

"You will never hear me coming, so I'm going to leave you with a little reminder Karl, a little something you will see every day when you look in the mirror."

Still holding him by his greasy hair, I placed the heel against his eye socket just to the side of his eye and pushed it into his flesh, then carved a half moon into his face. Blood drops splashed to the floor, as he groaned in pain.

"Karl, I only give a person one chance... Just one! I let go of his head and watched it fall to the wet bathroom floor with a small pool of blood beginning to form around his head. I pulled his wallet from the waist band of his French cut bathing suit and took a picture of his driver's license, 'click, click,' then showed it to him, and said, "I got ya Karl, so be a good boy..."

The cleaning girl was still outside, guarding the door for me. As I passed her, I slipped a hundred-dollar bill in her hand, never stopping. As I headed for the pool I glanced back to see her smile and put an 'out of service' sign on the door and roll her cart away. I quietly slipped into my Cabana from the back side, sat down and quickly put my red wig back into the case, nice and neat.

I sat reclined in the little love seat thing with my eyes closed for a moment, to savor the rush of pleasure filling me, shivers of electricity ran all over my skin. I sat up quickly and threw my ice water over my head, jolting me back to reality. I fluffed the wetness through my hair, gathered my things, let the white towel fall to the floor of the Cabana, then took my heels off and wiped the little blood drops off and dropped them into my pool bag, we don't want to leave any evidence, right! I walked out the front of the cabana.

Daphne was waiting for me, with a smile. I handed her my bag as we walked up to the hotel on our way to my room for a nap before dinner. I think I deserve one after my fun filled morning, practicing my skills, never underestimate the power of a psychological mind orgasm!

Chapter 17

A Date with a Killer!

'Security is mostly a superstition. It does not exist in nature, nor do the children of men as a whole experience it. Avoiding danger is no safer in the long run than outright exposure. Life is either a daring adventure, or nothing.'

Helen Keller

Evening came, and I was ready for a night of fun and food downstairs at the Blues in Biloxi Ball. The hotel was hosting it in the Grand Ballroom tonight. As I stepped out of the elevator, it was like I walked onto a Hollywood Red Carpet premiere. Except that for this Blues event the carpet was---blue, of course. The people going to the event were all dressed to the nines, with the newly arriving guests and other tourists standing outside the roped off entry snapping pictures, just like paparazzi. They added the perfect touch to the night's energy.

They planned this well, as it had the vibe of a real Hollywood event. I'm glad I had the hookup and got an invitation when I got here yesterday. I stood just outside the ropes watching the fun unfold, when a hand brushed my lower back as a man glided past me, with a nice gentle "Hello" the same hello as from the pool... It was him, holy-shit it's Collin. He is here! Holy shit, holy fucking shit. As he entered the doorway of the ballroom he glanced back with a smile---he was playing with me, unexpected to say the least.

Something I hadn't taken into consideration, is that he is a hunter as well; a very good and accomplished hunter, in fact. Has he been hunting me all this time? I've been busy with the FBI, Marshals, and the Romanian Mob. I didn't consider him, which could be dangerous, holy shit---I did get his attention that night at the party in New Orleans though.

How did he recognize me? I'm wearing a pure black straight cut wig, makeup, and gloves. I don't look anything like I did that night, how? Well maybe he is just hunting and doesn't realize it's me... How funny that would be. I walked in and headed right for the bar. I needed a drink and to get my mind orgasm on right now... He wasted no time at all, there he was standing in front of me with two champagne glasses.

"Have we met before?" he said with a smile.

I took one of the glasses and took a sip, "Only in my naughty dreams!" I shot back with a tantalizing grin...

His lips smiled slowly in self-appreciative amusement as he took the glass from my hand and at the same time placed his other on my lower back, while easing me right out onto the dance floor. This guy is very smooth, wow... And, of course, he could dance like a pro, I wouldn't expect anything less. I have to remember this is the guy that killed my sister and I'm returning the favor. Because I can see how a woman could lose herself with this guy.

"So, Toni tells me you love good music and great wine, or is it great music and good wine? What she didn't tell me is that you're into playing dress up...Unexpected... But nice! I happen to have an unpublished cut from Eric Gale's next album, in my room with a bottle of very nice wine chilling-- would you be interested?"

He smiled down deliberately into my eyes as if he were trying to hypnotize me with them... Creepy... and Sexy... but Damn… I could really get into this, that wouldn't be a good or a smart move for me right now. I had to play this just right to keep his attention on me and not disappear with him.

I looked up at him and said, "You're naughty." I could feel his eyes probing into me. He pulled me close and whispered in my ear, "Let's be naughty!" Then he gently began nibbling on my earlobe, soft light nibbles, sending prickle chills down my back. Wow, this guy is smooth and very dangerous!

I pushed him away and said, "How about we meet for breakfast, say 7am...?" I could see he didn't like the fact that I was strong enough to say no to him. His eyes turned black the second I said that. Collin just stood frozen, I leaned in and kissed his cheek, and went for his ear lobe, to let him know I was still interested, but I bit it and popped it drawing a trickle of blood.

He let out a soft gasp as I pulled back and licked my lips with his blood rolling down my chin. The look in his black eyes was carnivorously evil, but he liked it just the same. I smiled and walked towards the door, not looking back, hoping he was not following me and thank God, he wasn't!

Once in my room, I locked every lock on the door and even pushed the desk up against the door for more safety.

After shutting the curtains, I had to take a shower and wash his evil off me, you know that sense you get, something just isn't right about a person---this is that guy, black eyes and evil. I can see how women fall for him, but I did handle myself pretty good down there, right...?

Face to face with a killer and I stood my ground. I was feeling a little jazzed from the evening, so I made myself a cocktail from the mini bar and soon after I was out like a light. The next thing I remember was the phone ringing, waking me, "yes"?

The voice on the other end, said, "This is your wake up call, it's 6am, ma'am." I forgot I asked the front desk to call me. I wanted to be packed and be out the door ahead of him. About twenty minutes after the call the bellhop was knocking and off we went to the elevator together.

I wasn't about to walk down alone, he took my baggage to the front and I found a nice seat in the middle of the dining room and waited. The morning news was on TV above the bar, which caught my attention as they were talking about a murder that happened overnight near here, really near here... A young woman jogger was found along the Gulf shore, beaten, raped, and tied upside down on the walkway railing, on an upside down cross, her arms were outstretched alongside the Gulf. The Police had no leads at this time.

Of course, my mind went racing right to Collin, the timing, the elaborate display and I did turn him down last night! How long has this bastard been doing this? He kills a girl, negotiates a land deal and leaves without a trace, it makes sense, right? He does business deals all over the south. It's his perfect storm and nobody has put any of this together.

Except for me, I just have to prove it. I need some evidence for Jack.

Wait a minute. I'm in this to kill him, not solve the case for the FBI---just to kill him, right...?

Sticking to my plan is my sanity, my way out without mentally hurting myself, so I can go back to my lovely life in New Orleans and put all this behind me, the normal life, right...?

Normal---I know at this point, the deeper I go that may be easier said than done---let's see, the FBI, US Marshals, and the Romanian Gypsy Mob are all looking for me, yes, me, how crazy is that right...?

I keep asking myself that over and over---and then I see flashes of my sister hanging in that tree, and I remember why and now how many other women like the jogger this morning are there that he has done this to? These women and their families have no justice either. Collin has gotten away with abusing women, killing women, and it's his time to pay up. And I'm holding his card...!

Yes, I've thought about what this will do to me psychologically. Killing someone isn't normal, but then I have to think about the women and all their families. In a way, this is like war... what if I was a kind of soldier, a soldier fighting a war for women like my sister. I'm Lady Justice!

I'm fighting for her and all the other innocent women out there that have been abused by people like Collin. I'm more than sure there are a lot more of them than we think...!

Well it's 7:02 AM, and I don't see him. I guess killing that poor girl tired him out or whatever, I can't wait much longer, and Jean-Paul will be waiting for me.

"Good morning beautiful, sorry I'm late the shower would not heat up this morning." I smiled up at him and told him he owed me a Bloody Mary. He smiled and waved over the waiter. I eased back in my chair not knowing where this was going, but I know I will get my date out of this before I leave.

I asked him if he was hungry after last night's adventure. He looked at me with an unexpected look, he didn't know how to answer. "So, tell me about your evening, after I left you Collin?"

"Well, I went for a run and came back and showered, then fell into bed---that's about it."

He was fumbling with his napkin like a little school boy caught in a lie, how funny this is, I have a killer dancing on a hot plate...

"So, Collin, did the Police talk to you yet?" I said in passing.

"No, why would they need to talk to me?" he said while playing with his napkin again.

"Look, it's all over the news this morning, a girl was killed last night while jogging near here."

Collin was able to hold his facial expression as if he had no idea of what I was talking about. I could tell he was feeling the pressure though. I watched his carotid vein pump like an oil gusher. He was trying to work this out in his head and stay cool, but it wasn't working, so I changed the subject to his work.

"How is that land deal coming along you mentioned you were working on here in Mississippi?"

He smiled, then told me that he had a buyer for the new Casino project called 'Waterside' and they would break ground in the fall. He went on to tell me he was headed to a town in Florida, Sarasota, to work a deal for a new town project.

"My gosh, Collin, I have never been to Florida, I understand it's nice?" I said quizzically, as I grabbed his hand.

"Maybe I will get there someday and build something, who is doing the project?"

He put his coffee down and began telling me that his firm has contractors that they have worked with for years and are very happy with, but he could put in a good word for my firm to do the design work.

I said cagily, "But you haven't seen my work yet!"

"And you have not seen my work either!"

I returned with, "I believe I have seen your work!" I said with a look of repugnance. He sat there showing no emotion, just a blank look on his face, blank! This guy was in uncharted territory, an uncomfortable place. I just jolted the killer. He pulled out his notebook and jotted down an address and phone number explaining it was his number and the address of the airstrip he will be flying out of late today at three, and if I wanted to see Florida to be there.

Well, I guess I got my date with a killer... Right!

Chapter 18

New Orleans Queen of the Dead and the Mob!

'There are only the pursued, the pursuing, the busy and the tired.'

F. Scott Fitzgerald

"Lizzy, I haven't lost focus, or forgotten Sara and Raven, far from it. I want to know why that dirt bag was in the cabin at Alligator Bayou too. We need to see if all this is related to the case. If it is, then good for the Bureau, but my focus is on finding Sara's killer. Has Raven checked in with us lately? Asking anything?"

"Jack, that girl was hit hard at the scene---full blown seizures, just found her sister, and seeing what she saw---talk about splintered by trauma---that girl won't be right for a long while..." said Lizzy.

"Yeah, I got that, Lizzy. I fucked up and took her there, I know that, and I have to deal with that."

Outside three SUV's pulled up with all the Port players in cuffs. EJ, along with the CRT squad, were surrounding the trucks with their guns up and ready. They did a visual check of the area before dragging the men out of the vehicles. Bobby positioned himself in the rear of the squad to watch for any movement. He had two of his snipers positioned high and out of sight, just in case. They didn't know who they could really trust, but his team was ready to take anyone down if they made a move.

EJ led the men up the steps to the door. As the team filtered in with the men and went up the steps, and were getting them ready for entry into the Port office, EJ had been listening to her radio. She knew what Jack needed her to do as they entered the doorway. She grabbed Gardner by the arm and suddenly a shot rang out hitting the glass window of the door, shattering it into EJ's face, everyone hit the ground and returned fire, at what they didn't know---Bobby called out to his snipers to see who had the gunman? A single shot rang out, as Bobby heard "shooter down sir, you're in the clear."

Bobby yelled to the squad---"Move, move now---get them inside!"

EJ burst through the door, dragging Gardner like a dog straight into the room they had ready. As they rounded the corner---Gardner had a smile on his face, but that seemed to leave him, replaced with frantic gloom when he saw the two officers cuffed to chairs as they approached the room. He dropped his head and slowed his steps, trying to fight back as EJ, still bleeding from the glass from the door, grabbed his neck pulling him close, "Can you feel your butt hole tightening, dumb ass?" as she wiped the blood to the side with her sleeve and gave him a jerk as they entered the room. "That bullet was meant for you, asshole!" said EJ.

Gardner couldn't take his eyes off Captain Pitchley, knowing what Pitchley knew about the operation at the Port and the Den. Everything was in jeopardy now. No one was safe from the Den, no one!

EJ forced him into the chair and slammed him down, bouncing his head on the desk, then cuffed his ankles to the bottom of the chair, reached up and wrenched both his arms behind him and cuffed them to the back of the chair as well.

She left him with a "Sit tight, rat," and walked out grabbing the door behind her. She gave Jack the nod, and went to get the rest of the crew of bad guys waiting just outside the bullpen door. Jack was on the other side of the room talking to the other Unit Chiefs as to the situation, and about Captain Pitchley and the Lieutenant. These guys were caught off guard for sure...

Jack told them they needed to get started on the questioning before Justice and I.A. showed up. He made his way over to the room with Gardner waiting in it. As he passed the Captain, Jack slapped him on the shoulder and told him, "By the way, you won't be going anywhere soon, Pitchley---isn't that a Romanian name?" smiled Jack. "I just saw that name in a book, titled Masquerade Inc. How funny! But not for you..."

Jack walked in the interrogation room and closed all the blinds, then walked over to Gardner and pulled out a cloth from his back pocket and gagged him with it. Gardner's eyes held a flash of shock as Jack leaned in close and said, "Now, we don't want you to spoil our fun, do we!"

With a very loud tone, Jack began talking aloud, so Pitchley could hear every word..."We have your books and the store, Masquerade, so you haven't got much left to bargain for here." Jack walked over to the door and stood as he finished his speech, "I want names, numbers, safe houses, and of course the inner workings of the Den..."

Still standing at the door, shots started flying through the windows of the office, glass exploding in all directions---Jack hit the floor to return fire when he heard shots outside and saw Pitchley falling through the window opening of the office, hanging there, dead from several gun shots to the head and chest. Lizzy and Bobby had to take him down.

Jack ran over to Gardner, but he was gone as well---two lucky shots to the head. Jack just slid to the floor in disbelief and shouted, "Shit, how did that happen?"

"Jack, Pitchley had an ankle holster! Are you ok?" yelled Lizzy.

"Well, we are now fucked, Justice will shut us down for sure." said Jack in a shallow tone.

Lizzy reached out to pull Jack to his feet as the outside door burst open. In walked a team of U.S. Marshals like they owned the place. Everyone in the room turned as they reached for their weapons, still a little tense from the shooting.

"Who is the agent in charge of this cowboy circus?" one of the Marshals shouted. The entire room fell silent, all looking in Jack's direction.

Jack stood up and brushed glass off himself as he and Lizzy walked over to the men. D just kept typing on his keyboard like he was the only one in the room. He did have a curious gaze with a raised eyebrow. D knew Jack was probably in hot water, but he also knew Jack had a way of turning things around on a dime, or in his case a rusty penny. He had used the other nine cents over the years.

The men and Lizzy stepped into the empty interrogation room and shut the door. The silent room of law enforcers snapped back into action with two dead bodies to work up and reports to do.

 Inside the room one of the Marshals yanked his sunglasses off and began to scream at Jack; "You just got our number one suspect killed, before we could take him down, so now we have no informant and no idea what is going to happen to our investigation."

Jack's head now tilted, just to the right, like a dog ready for a biscuit---and spoke up with calm focused tone, "Informant, you said two words, suspect and informant, who are you talking about Marshall, Gardner or Sara? Yes, we know about Sara!"

The Marshall looked back at Jack with a sheepish kind of look, and said in a very low monotone voice; "Sara Rossinoff, we had her in the WITSEC program in exchange for information on the Romanian Mob and the Den."

Jack's head snapped around and words just came flying out... "You mean Sara from New Orleans, Sara dead in a tree, that SARA?" ranted Jack.

"Yes, we have had her in the program for three years and were about to move in on the operation, when we lost contact with her a few days ago. Then she came up as part of your investigation at Alligator Bayou."

The Marshals eyes were down and to the right---with the vein in his neck thumping like a gusher as he spoke. Jack knew he was back in the driver's seat again and threw up his finger and said, hold that thought---as he made his way to the door. Lizzy just turned to the foggy window overlooking the Port and shook her head in amazement, then told the men to take seats, they were going to be a while, and asked, "Who is your Boss?"

She threw in a "Thank you gentlemen. You're idiots, but thank you." She knew Jack's ass was in the clear and he had all he needed to move on all of this and keep the Port shut down. He was also hopeful this would help Raven.

Jack walked over to Domingo and filled him in on the short version, then flagged EJ and Bobby over, filling both of them in on the new old plan for the Bayou case. Thanks to the U.S. Marshals information. Jack then made the announcement to the room that the Port stayed shut until he cleared it. The room went into an uproar, and Jack just stood there with a smile on his face.

"Quiet, we will have a brief in one hour. Let us know when Justice and I.A. are here---I want them in the lunch room and only them. Bobby will have CRT at the door and Swat will cover the outside, am I clear?"

On the other end of the room the Police Commissioner yelled back "What about us? Who do you think you are, agent? These are my men and my town!"

Jack stopped and looked his way and said; "Commissioner, with all due respect, the Captain and the Lieutenant are your men too. This has now turned into a Justice investigation, and we have jurisdiction and will be handling it. Thank you, and by the way, your department is under investigation as well, so take a seat."

The men couldn't do anything but hang their heads in disgrace and follow directions. Jack knew he had them all by the balls, and when you have them by the balls, you've got the power...

Jack walked over to Bobby and told him, "If Justice gives you any push back about being put in the room, tell them it's for their safety." Bobby nodded as he made his way over to his team to brief them. Jack took a minute to collect his thoughts before going back at the Marshals, while Lizzy came out of the room to see how Jack was going to attack the situation.

"Well, JB, you really do have nine lives. This was a fucked-up mess, and now you can have just about anything you need," said Lizzy.

"Well, kiddo, we hopefully have the missing pieces to pull all this together, and we were right---it's all related, thank God!" exclaimed Jack with relief.

Jack put his hand on Lizzy's shoulder and said, "Let's go eat some Marshals for lunch," as they made their way to the room.

Lizzy popped the door open, and Jack walked right in and over to Domingo and asked what he had so far.

"Well, they filled in some blanks and Jack, we have the address of her apartment. They have been letting her have some freedoms, so to speak." D looked up from his computer screen and winked at Jack.

"Freedoms? What does he mean gentlemen---please explain freedoms," asked Jack.

The Marshals looked at each other, and really didn't want to speak, when Jack reminded them this was now his investigation and Justice was right outside waiting for a briefing.

"Gentlemen, the only way this is going to work at this point, is by you telling us the truth and I mean the whole truth, guys. We figured out Sara was into some weird shit that her sister had no idea of," explained Jack.

"Wait a minute, sister? What are you talking about?" one of the Marshals asked.

Jack's eyes narrowed, and he said, "You don't know about the sister? Well, gentlemen, Raven Rousseau, the Architect---she lives in New Orleans, just off Canal Street. Her picture was in Sara's car. Boys, this is getting interesting," said Jack.

"When did she make contact with her sister, Jack?" said the Marshal.

"Two weeks ago, yesterday. That's what we discovered in the interview." said Domingo while looking at Lizzy with a questionable look.

Lizzy walked over to Jack to ask him something, when the door opened, and Bobby stepped in and gave Jack the nod... Lizzy slapped Jack on the shoulder and left with Bobby. She was going to start the briefing for Justice who already had seen the reporter out front broadcasting as planned.

"Ok, our deal with Sara was that she stayed in the ring and finished gathering the information we needed to bring the whole operation down, internationally."

"Because of that, she had to appear to be doing business as usual, Jack," said the Marshal.

"What business was she doing besides getting herself killed for ratting out the organization, boys?" voiced Jack.

"Jack, she was an internet Gothic Dominatrix---had been since her early teen years, Jack---you didn't know? Man---she was one messed up girl, Jack. We have hours and hours of tape on how her parents, friends and the Den leaders themselves would use her and other girls for their sadistic camp meetings." That's what she called them---she called them camp meetings at the Bayou cabins where you found her. I mean wild shit, Jack."

Jack fell back in a chair, and was silent for a moment. Everyone was silent for a moment... Domingo asked for the tapes and asked where she did her other stuff. When Jack stood back up and said, "You guys put her up in an apartment and let her do this, right?... I mean if you were smart you would have bugged the place and put cameras in too, right?"

"Yes, we did, but they went black a day before Sara disappeared," uttered the embarrassed Marshal.

"You think you might have checked on her when they went black---you know, to protect your investment and all... We need those tapes too, and Marshal, you're writing me a detailed report with all this in it, understand!" snapped Jack.

"That's not all, Jack. We began hearing from some of our other CI's in the area that the Romanian Mob Boss was looking for someone. We thought it was Sara, but she was dead... So, we don't have anything but a description of the girl they are hunting. Jack, they have a half-a-mill bounty on this person's head. According to our people, she beat the shit out of him, and stabbed him in the shoulder out in front of his club in New Orleans," said the Marshals, as Jack walked over to Domingo.

About then Lizzy entered the room and said, "Well, that went fine Jack. They are giving you an open ticket---but said you better get the guy and they better be able to shut the group down. I'm to keep them updated. And, as for you boys, you are to give us everything we need including working with our team back in the city, got it?"

One said, "Yes ma'am," when Jack looked up and asked them where they thought they were going. Then Jack told them to wait outside and we would all be heading to the apartment together. Jack walked into the other room and told EJ to take over and have Bobby help her with the interrogations---and to "be sure to stay with the live feeds so we know what you have when you get it."

"By the way, gentlemen, what was that description of the person the Romanian Mod is hunting?" said Jack as they headed towards the doorway.

"Well, female, five foot nine, taller with spiked heels, white face, dark eyes, tight leather pants and corset top, blood red lips, black hair in a cropped face kind of hair do."

"Marshal, you just described the Gothic Queen of the Dead, here in New Orleans, and how are we supposed to react? I don't know about you, but I'm thinking about taking away your gun and drug testing you!"

"Is her sister the Voodoo Queen out there also...? Do you get my drift, Marshal? You can't ID this person, other than female---are you even sure about that, considering again, we are in New Orleans?"

"No, not really at this point, sir." said the Marshal.

"Ok, guys, take that description to all the underground bars and tattoo places along with the sketch, see if anyone can help---and not laugh in your faces, it's not much, but it's all we have. I need my team to get eyes on her apartment---do you have a problem with that Marshal, shaking his head... Queen of the dead...?" said Jack.

"No sir, but she was at Sara's place the day before yestraday." said the Marshal...

"WHAT, she was in Sara's apartment?" Jack asked.

"Jack, she got away before I could get any information---she ran..."

Chapter 19

Dinner and Common Ground!

'It feels quite cool, in a mad way, to be someone who sculls about in the shadows.'

Peter Bayham

Jean-Paul was right there at the front door waiting for me. He smiled as I walked up. He grabbed my bags and opened my door for me like I was someone important. I jumped in and off we went... He looked back and asked if I had a good time relaxing?

I looked up with a sheepish grin and said, "You didn't get a report of my naughtiness, Mr. Cabby?" He smiled and made a stop at a red light.

"Where am I taking the Queen of New Orleans?" he asked.

I looked up at him through the rear-view mirror and said, "A nice hotel in the Quarter my good man...!" Then I slid down in my seat and closed my eyes, giving some thought to my plans for my date with Collin.

I could feel Jean-Paul watching me from the mirror. I'm glad I have him with me, someone to almost trust, yes, almost. People will always fail you at some point, always---it's their nature! I fell asleep, a deep sleep too. I seem to do that with him and in his cars---go figure. I haven't, or I should say don't, sleep well now with all I have going on. I guess my subconscious knows I feel safe with Jean-Paul around.

We reached the Quarter and he pulled up to the Hotel Royal, an 1827 Creole Townhouse. I sat up, stretched, and told him, "This was a great pick, Mr. Cabby, hiding me in plain sight---timeless," I remarked.

"Be careful, and don't dress in the outfit you wore that night, please." He had a look of concern all over his face.

"I will be a good girl, and I know you have people watching me here, don't you?" I said, as I put my very large floppy hat on and bounced out of the car.

"Of course, I do---we must keep you safe. Do you like my new car?" Jean-Paul changed the subject pretty quickly. He doesn't know I have figured him out, and know the whole story, but that's ok for now, a girl needs a good bodyguard from time to time.

"Yes, I love it, you must be doing well in New Orleans, and with the Faksyon here in the South." Then I disappeared into the lobby of the Royal. I could hear JP laughing madly out on the sidewalk.

I did a spin around, to check this lovely place out. It was perfect for my tastes, old and beautifully crisp. The woman behind the desk looked up and asked if she could help me. She was Creole as could be.

I love that little accent mixed with English. I told her I was here for a visit and needed a room with a street view, and would like a bottle of champagne as well. I watched as her eyebrow arched and the words started to come---

"I sorry, ma'am, we don't hav..." That's as far as she got. I could feel Jean-Paul walk up behind me.

"Our best room is ready for you, ma'am, and I will have Peter bring you a chilled bottle of champagne. Do you want it in the room or on your balcony, ma'am?" I'm beginning to just love when that happens. I turned and smiled at Jean-Paul. I could tell he was lost at what just happened, but I love doing it, it's just fun---he does just reign fear in these people.

"I guess we need to talk, don't we?" he asked as we walked to the steps. I smiled and said dinner in the courtyard would be nice, at six? He nodded and up we went. I unpacked and washed my face, put on a hotel robe and strolled out to the balcony where a nice glass of champagne was waiting for me. I took a minute for myself and sat sipping slowly with my eyes closed taking in the smells of the city. I love my city. I can always feel an energy in me when I'm here. Even though, I have to be more selective where I go now, after all, I'm in Europe grieving.

But we have my sister to thank for her gothic wild side and many costumes and wigs, to keep me safe in the shadows. As I sat reflecting on my plan for Collin, a horse drawn carriage rolled by, the click clack of the horse's metal shoes striking the cobblestones was like fine music to my ears. Then the sound of a sweet saxophone came popping out of the place across the street, followed by a crack of thunder.

Click clack, more saxophone, and more pops of thunder, it was like a concert, as I made my way in to get dressed for dinner and a talk with Jean-Paul. The soft sounds of rain began and thunder in the distance. Nature was setting the tone for our meeting in the shadows.

I made it down before he got there. I sat with my back to the entrance, very brave I thought. I choose the blue dress, white heels and my white floppy hat, my Jackie O look to shield my identity, and my black cropped wig to complete the look... A crisp sixties with a dash of Goth look--- I call it my Jackie G style. I could hear footsteps behind me, I placed my hand on the butter knife just in case...

"Well, I see you have chosen the Blue tonight, how inviting you are," he said as he bowed and sat down.

"Yes, I'm a nightmare, dressed like a dream..." as I sipped my champagne. It feels quite cool, in a mad way, to be someone who sculls about in the shadows, right... I love those quotes.

"Well, where do I begin? Life has been written with so many chapters, it's hard now, to just tell my story."

I looked up at him and simply said, "The beginning will do, you're safe with me."

He looked down at the table, and picked up his water and sipped, then cleared his throat. "It all began back in Haiti when I was a teen. "

"I walked into the government office one day and told them, I'm here to be a soldier! They looked at me and told me to go home."

"I wasn't very happy at that point if you could imagine... so I turned my anger into a plan and found six other teens, like me, mad at what was happening around us and began talking to them about what we could do to change things. They thought I was crazy at first, but when I showed up one day with three rifles and two hand guns, they started to listen. It's funny actually, how easy it was to take power over them."

"To the south of the capital city, was a Faction of men and women fighting the government soldiers, and I was intent on stopping them for the government, thinking that would help me become a soldier. But things have a way of working out in different ways than you expect, wouldn't you agree…? You either have to follow them, or take another road. I took that other road, as you will see."

"One afternoon, we were watching the movements of the top leaders and one of them came close to where I was hiding, and I took him by knife point---we quietly got him back to our little hideout in the city, and I began interrogating him. I began with a hammer and his left knee. To this day I don't know what or how all this came over me, but it did and when I was done he had given me all the information I needed to take back to the government. I had the group's plans for attacks on armor storage buildings, government rallies, and even the President's home."

"By the end of the next day, I was with the head of the President's secret police, the MVSN. He wanted more, and told me I had a gift for this. He told me to set up a place in the city, and he would pay me and my men to gather this information. As you can imagine my head was spinning."

"My meeting was with Luckner Cumbronne, head of the Milice de Valuntaires de la S'ecurite, and he only answered to the President himself. He is the man who enlisted me and my men. You can only imagine what that did to a young man like me. I was a Lieutenant in the MVSN, I had a purpose."

"I began sitting in on some of their interrogations, but they soon learned that I was more efficient and effective than they were. So, you can see how fast I rose in the organization. Within months I was Major Archilles, head of the President's interrogators squad. I only reported to the President himself as well."

"Raven, I had my own little secret. I was on a trip to Bogotá for a fishing job I did a couple of years ago before the MVSN, when I stumbled onto a group of, well, let's say criminals, to be nice. They had this business card ruse they used on tourists. I had an opportunity to talk to one of the younger ones at a bar, and he introduced me to (Devil's Breath), a natural grown drug by the name, Scopolamine. It is a white powder that, blown into the face, or if the person just touches the edge of the business card with the powder on it they become totally compliant to whatever you ask them---lack of free will."

"The victim is powerless to recall events or identity perpetrators the next day. It was the perfect interrogation tool. And believe me, I capitalized on it, in secret of course. We began a friendship and an on-going business deal, to supply me with all I needed for my work. As you can imagine, my business was good, very good. No one ever knew my secret, which made me a very mysterious figure, wouldn't you say?"

"Then everything in Haiti started to go south, and I went north to your country. I have used this time to slowly build the Faksyon. I see it as the protection of my people. I know some see it as a gang, or us as criminals."

"Raven, we are building a nation within a nation, like the Latin's have done all these years. Do people get hurt from time to time---yes, it is necessary---something you see as true now. Raven, my people have more here than they ever could have there, and the women are not in fear of the men hurting or raping them. Something else I know you can identify with, I believe?"

He was so very right, I thought to myself. I just stared into the lion fountain behind him as I smiled. I told him about the day the FBI took me to see the place where my sister was murdered. That I had no idea she was still there hanging in that tree, but they took me anyway. "Jean-Paul, that was the moment a switch flipped in my head and deep in my soul, very deep in my now dark, empty soul. I also was sure someone would pay for what they had done to my sister, and that I knew I was the one that would avenge her and the other women this guy had killed."

Jean-Paul just sat and listened, not saying anything. His face---I could feel his eyes searching my face for sadness.

I asked him what he thought, and he said, "Raven, you have been hurt very deeply, and I must tell you that, that may have been what you needed to really find yourself, and what you are meant to do in this cruel world---you too may have a cause to fight for now. Do you think he, this one man, is the only killer out there hurting young women? He is not, Raven. There are so many more, and in this very city alone, your city, Raven. Take a long look into yourself and think about these past days and weeks---you are very good at this revenge game. It seems to come naturally like my gifts I told you about. Raven, you make a great Queen of New Orleans or Lady Justice, whichever you think fits you."

I looked right though him at the Lion waterfall on the wall behind him and thought about his words. *Was he right, or am I just about to become a common murderer myself...?*

Chapter 20

Crash Course

I love fairy tales because of their haunting beauty and magical strangeness. They are set in worlds where anything can happen. Frogs can be kings, a thicket of brambles can hide a castle where a royal court has lain asleep for a hundred years, a boy can outwit a giant, and a girl can break a curse with nothing but her courage and steadfastness.

Kate Forsyth

The place was a mess, as I entered Sara's apartment. The Marshals had been here picking the place apart for days now; tape pieces for finger prints all over the floor; different colors of dust in spots all around the room, on walls and, look at that, even on the bedroom ceiling. Drawers dumped, clothes thrown everywhere--- "What the hell man, these guys are cowboys." Lizzy just stood there looking at me as I got that crazy look in my eyes and began to ball my fist.

"Ok Marshals, out, out now! We need the room," said Lizzy.

Lizzy walked over to me and we began (talking) the room together, step by step, as we made our way into the bedroom, when Domingo walked in behind us, laughing at what he saw. I turned and pointed him right to the video cam in the next room. Domingo headed in to take it apart and hopefully find us something...

Lizzy took the bedroom closet, and just had to stop for a second in front of the swing bed, before moving on to the closet---Lizzy had that bizarre look on her face. I couldn't help but think, *what was this girl's broken deal? Those two sisters were like night and day.*

I could hear Lizzy making all sorts of comments from the closet, ending with, "Jack, you have <u>got</u> to see all this." I turned to head that way, when I noticed a small necklace hanging from the lamp on the side table. I had seen it somewhere, but couldn't place it. Lizzy caught my attention with a snap of a whip she picked up in the secret closet.

"Really Lizzy, your old habits coming back, are they?" I said in a fun tone.

"Wow, don't you wish, JB... This girl was a ball of unexpected, right Jack?" Lizzy said with a smile.

"She was your kind of girl, wild, spirited, doing her own thing, her way, so to speak, but what a broken mess, Lizzy. We have seen this kind of thing before, but holy God...," Jack said as he shook his head in astonishment.

"Ok, Jack, we know she was in WITSEC and informed on the organization to Justice, who was supposed to be taking down the organization, but didn't seem to be getting to that, right?" asked Lizzy.

"Lizzy, according to the Marshals, they needed more on the international part of the organization before they would move!"

"Why? That falls outside of their purview."

I took a few steps in and looked over all the costumes, makeup and toys. Toys was an understatement, she must have had every possible sex and S.M. gadget you could buy---this poor girl, what gives? How does this happen? It would take years of experience to be at this level in this world. At what age did this start?

"You're right, Jack, why more internationally, as they put it. The Marshals, as with us, are domestic agencies---it doesn't make sense. What if they stumbled onto some high-ranking shit they couldn't let go of?" asked Lizzy.

"Fine, Lizzy, but why twist and tie this girl up so much. Well, that didn't sound right---I'm sorry!"

"Someone, somewhere, had a hard-on for this girl!" said Lizzy.

"Who and why? Hey D, have you got anything we can put together yet---we need it, buddy." said Jack.

"Well, Jack, they had this place well-wired and an outgoing router that landed at a feed close to here, actually. I can't bring it up, but we can walk over there to see what we find, guys?"

"Walk, no shit?" laughed Lizzy.

"No shit, boys and girls," said Domingo.

We hit the door, and told our CRT guy to not let *anyone* in this place---we would be back shortly. D was right---it was literally across the street, and up two flights of stairs in a room that looked right at her apartment---like some spy shit you see on TV. Lizzy put a foot to the door and we were in. The place was a maze of wires and servers, with a couple of monitors near the windows facing the street. Whoever they were, they saw everyone going in or out of this place.

D jumped in and tried to bring up some of the recordings and find out who these creeps were. I did notice a bad sign over in corner on a small dining table---empty coffee cups and pizza boxes---this just got very domestic, not foreign, I called Lizzy over and showed her my find. She jumped on the phone and called for some of our scene guys to get over here and run some DNA---bad move on them, so much for high level shit.

They had messed up and given us a leg up, and I was running with it. My hunch was Marshals and local PD mixed in on a great sex scheme they could run.

I grabbed for my phone, when Lizzy yelled, "Over here, Jack. I found this under the cabinet lip in the kitchen---it is a list of names with pictures attached to each page. I recognize some of these ole boys, Jack... That is the Mayors right hand guy, and our beloved Congressman, and look, Police Chief Rollins himself and many more. All tied up being whipped and diapered Jack, really diapered..."

"Well, Liz, it takes a big man to be diapered like a baby to be able to run this city... Remember this is crazy town New Orleans."

Jack, get over here. I got the piece you both are missing---these cowboys were being played, and Jack, being played big---this sounds like the Romanians on the Russian side were watching and listening to everything, and definitely pulling the strings. I can't make out what they were saying, but in the background of these recordings are conversations all in Romanian, I think."

"Lizzy, call EJ and Bobby, I want them to take Lieutenant Asshole Colter to a nice place and have an---EJ kind of talk with him," Jack snapped.

"I want all he has on Sara and the Den. Have Bobby get two of his best guys to help run point. We need it done now. I want to know what this girl has to do with them, and why they had to kill her."

"Jack, it looks like she knew every aspect of the operation and all the players---she had to die!"

"Even though I'm sure she had evidence on them? Then---why would they risk it? Jack we are missing something here."

"Well, you don't kill the person that has the dirt on you, unless they didn't do this, and we are really looking for someone else. Lizzy, we need..."

"I'm on it already, Jack, all the file work and case notes. I will have all the parishes report in on any cases like ours, to see if we can get a match."

"With the body displayed as elaborate as that---this isn't the first one..."

"Jack, what about EJ and Bobby, still want them to press the Lieutenant?"

"Hell, yes, Lizzy, we need all the information we can get---there is still a connection there somehow, I just feel it."

"Be back in a second, Jack, I'll have D patch us in with them as they move on this, ok?" said Lizzy.

"Thanks."

Back at Sara's apartment, I moved deeper into the closet of pure mystery---or hell, I haven't figured that out yet. All I know is this is some deep warped psychology shit, one sister very vanilla, the other sister dark chocolate for sure.

"Hey D, you got anything out there?" I shouted.

"Well---yes, but Jack, it's a little twisted. JB, you're really not going to like it!" Domingo said as he stood on a small ladder with his head stuck up in the ceiling.

"Ok, lay it on me D... What did you find?"

"Ok Jack, there are no live feeds here at the moment, but there is an outside feed that smells all Marshal to me if you get my drift. I believe they have been watching Sara with a separate feed for a while---if she was under witness protection, then why would they have her working as usual, Jack?"

"That's twisted, don't you think, and they sure didn't volunteer the information or video feed to us, did they." smiled Domingo.

"Fucking Marshals, this shit just gets deeper and deeper. How far and how high will this shit go? EJ needs to break that guy and get names for us!"

"I'm on it, JB, we are almost to the site now, and Bobby is there setting up for me with his guys. I will be live in twenty," she explained.

"Great, I forgot we were a live feed, nice---do your thing---no stones unturned!"

"EJ, remember these guys are hardened Eastern European thugs, go at him hard and I don't give a damn if he is wearing blue or not..." said Jack.

"Done, JB, I brought my little box of fun with me, got me?" EJ clicked off.

I walked over to the swinging bed and sat on the edge to think for a second, still eyeing that necklace, I know I have seen it before. Shit, I was tired. I fell back onto the bed and closed my eyes, and out I went.

 Suddenly Bobby came over the com with - "Hold, hold on your position, EJ. We've got company here at the cabin. There are two black limousines flanked by a black SUV. We have eyes on the old man from the boathouse, talking to four men dressed in black from head to toe. Two have assault rifles, Jack---these have to be your mob guys---we are running the plates and are sitting just out of range, Jack."

"Snap pictures of every move, get us some faces we can use. Can we get them followed when they leave, Bobby?"

"I already called for the chopper to tail them quietly as they leave. Jack. These guys have balls to do a meeting right after we leave the place, while it's under investigation, don't you think?"

"Not when you think you have the Police in your pocket, and possibly the Marshals. These guys are from Eastern Europe remember..."

"You know, balls for brains, what's my move, JB?"

"Stay still, unless they move on the old man. I want to have a conversation with that man! He is involved in this shit..."

"Jack, I don't think we should use the cabin for my conversation, do you?" said EJ.

"Actually, I still want you to do it there, and I want the old man to know it---catch what I'm saying? Bobby, get more of your guys down there too."

"I read your mind, Jack---Roscoe and his team will touch down in less than twenty," said Bobby.

"Where has he been? I noticed he wasn't with you," said Jack.

"His wife just had another son---that's four little Roscoe's this world has to deal with, right..?" laughed Bobby.

"Shit, they just hit the old man, he's down Jack---should I move? I have them in my sights...they won't know what hit them---do I have the go?" urged Bobby.

Chapter 21

Blind Justice

'Don't ever empty the bucket of mystery. Never let people define what you do. It's not about zigging when you should zag. It's not about something unpredictable. It's just about never being a word, or something that is not in the process of transforming.'

Marilyn Manson

We finished dinner about 7:30 or so. Jean-Paul got up, kissed my hand and told me to get some rest tonight. That I would be safe here, he was watching. I smiled without looking at him, as I continued to watch the waterfall drip water into the small pool at the floor.

I must have sat alone watching that little waterfall for well over ten minutes before the waitress asked me if I needed anything. I looked over at her, "yes, please send a fresh chilled bottle of Champagne to my balcony, please."

"Yes ma'am, would you like a cheese and meat plate or fruit?" she asked

"No, not tonight, but thank you," I replied as I got up and headed to the stairway to my room. I walked in and dropped my dress and shoes on the floor in front of the bed and reached for the robe I had on earlier. I looked in the mirror at myself for a second thinking about those words...*Revenge, Vengeance, Murder, Justice, right from wrong, and am I crazy?*

The sounds of jazz from the street broke my thoughts and I walked over to the railing and watched the little street band stroll by playing a light, cool jazz melody. I heard the door open behind me, as the waitress from downstairs walked in with my Champagne and set it on the table for me. I handed her a five and a smile.

She nodded, and then left. The band had passed, and I was left with a quiet view of the street now. I sat and put my legs up on the railing while I sipped the bubbles. I know someone is going to pay for what they did to my sister, and I do know I'm the one who has to do it. That is the only right thing that is happening.

I have changed my views on a few things in life for sure---I'm not the same girl I was just before seeing my sister in that tree. That girl was nice, sweet and naive to Sara's world, an architect for God's sake. I would hear a news report about such things from time to time, but I was distanced from that as we all are. Sara was in the shadows every day, as are so many other women out there at the hands of such bad people.

Well, bad men---who need to be dealt with for sure. Sara almost told me the story, but now I'm left to figure it out for myself. That vision I was having the night Professor Taylor was carrying me, as I bounced lightly in his arms as he walked up the deck. There was something there, foggy but important. A strange room, it was the cabin---I can see that, but who were all the people standing all around.

I poured myself another glass and sat with my eyes closed trying to pull those old flashes from my head, something Mary tried with me in some of the sessions we had. She tried to pull the old memories, it was called Cognitive something, and she would have me close my eyes and think back to memories and tell her what I was seeing in my head. Thinking back---but there was nothing there. Mary did try to get into my childhood from time to time, but I would instantly change the topic and run off at the mouth about something else. I guess that's my way of shutting down pain. Mary's play at cognitive therapy didn't really have a chance.

So that does have something to say about where my subconscious really has been all along...? It would seem the mysterious Queen of New Orleans may have been in there, growing, maturing, and learning all this time, like Jean-Paul told me. And it took Sara to wake her up---that would explain the mind orgasms I get---my memory working to come out. This is some wild psych shit---Mary would be proud of me.

I looked to the street below and saw a shadow of a person standing in a doorway across the street. I couldn't make out who it was, but they were watching me for sure. I eased my phone out from my pocket and called Jean-Paul, to ask him if it was one of his men watching over me.

"Hey, do you have a guy watching me from across the street of the hotel?"

He paused, then said, "I'm sending a car, don't move."

"Not a problem, I'm ready---Jean, if he is not one of yours I need to have a talk with him! Got me?"

"Yes ma'am I do..." It was like you could hear a smile on his face when I said that.

I knew it wasn't the police, they didn't have me on their radar...yet! This guy was probably a mob guy---if so, I may have an issue. Out of literally nowhere, two black cars zipped in front of the shadowy figure and four other shadowy figures from both sides of the street surrounded this guy and grabbed him, then threw him in the back of one of the cars and sped off---while someone else knocked on my door.

I looked through the peephole thing to see Jean standing there. I raced to unlock it and let him in. As I did he said, "Get dressed, and let's go."

I ran into the bedroom and threw on some clothes and a wig, just in case. I could hear him talking to someone in Creole, then laughter rang out.

"Raven, this guy is a low-level informant for the mob---a really low-level guy---he doesn't even have a cell phone!!" he said while laughing.

"I still want to have a word with him, Jean.."

"I don't think that is a good idea---when this guy turns up missing, which he will, I don't need you involved in any way, understand?"

"Well, look at it this way, we need to establish a presence, and what better way than to send them a message from *the Faksyon*," I said.

"Ok, I like your thinking, but it's too early in the game to do that---you need to finish your little game with Collin first. Get what I'm saying, Raven?"

"Fine then, all a girl wanted was to get a little information out of him."

"That's my department, while keeping you safe---we are going to move you," Jean ordered.

"Hey, I have a better idea. I will meet Collin for that trip to Florida he asked me about. That gets me out of the way for awhile," I said with a smile.

Jean didn't say a word for a couple of seconds---but you could see he was working something out in his head when he asked,

"Do you know where in Florida you're going?"

I told him Sarasota. He picked up his phone and walked out onto the balcony to talk. I poured myself a glass of whiskey from the bar, and sat down on the sofa. He was out there for a while talking. I listened but couldn't understand him. I do love the sound of their language. I think it's the pieces of French that pop out from time to time.

Jean came in from the balcony and sat in the chair across from me and said the funniest thing, "Ok, you can go to Florida!," as we both busted out in laughter.

Then he took out a pad of paper and pen and began writing, "This is the number you call for any help you may need once you touch down in Sarasota, his name is John-Pillar, John-Pillar Bellebranche. He is my guy down there. I have him working at the new Westin---he is the Concierge there. We have about ten more on staff as well. Do you know where he has you staying?"

"No, he doesn't know I'm actually coming yet. I have to meet him at the airport in the morning," I said with an uncertain smile, which he picked up on right away.

"You have some reservations about this?" he asked.

"You picked up on that, I see," as I got up from the sofa to pour myself another Whisky. "I'll be fine!" I said with a slight bit of cracking in my voice.

"Would you prefer that I go and stay in the background for you? This is a dangerous guy, Raven!"

"No, I will be just fine, I'm a big girl with a big mission!"

"Raven, I could just end this for you and we could get back to business as usual. Just think, tomorrow you could walk into your office and say hi to everyone, and go to lunch and tell them all about your time in Europe. Drink wine and enjoy," he said with a little bit of sarcasm in his voice.

I sat there, looking him right in the eyes, and said, "You might be right, but I have to do this for myself, or I will never be the same---I can't explain it now. It's this force in me, I can't stop---there are a lot of women and families that need peace. I can give that to them."

"Collin has been killing for a long time, Jean, and those families need some peace, and it has to be at my hands, my way... I can't explain it to you, but this has to be done."

"No, Raven, I do understand, every part of this---I had my mission, and no one stood in my way, remember?" he said as his phone rang and he got up to answer it.

I walked out to the balcony, when I noticed Peter, little Peter, sitting on the door stoop across the street. He waved and I smiled back and waved. It was nice to know I was being looked after so well.

"Jean, little Peter is a nice touch, thank you."

"He asked to be here for you. You must have made a good impression on Peter---he has never taken to anyone at all. I have known him for years, he's one of my best. I can know you're safe if he is anywhere around."

"Thank you..." I said in a deep southern drawl, playing with him.

Jean left shortly after that, and I ran myself a bath to relax. I needed to get my head in the game and get ready for tomorrow and all that it might bring.

Morning broke, five a.m. I was up and out. Peter drove me to the private airport that Collin was flying out of this morning. Much to my surprise, he was not there yet. I took this as a good thing---this gave me the element of surprise, and I took it. A young man took my bag and asked if I needed anything. I told him I was fine, and not to tell Collin I was aboard, that I wanted to be a surprise.

He smiled and said, "No problem." As I sat in one of the very nice cushy leather seats, I noticed a car flying in. It was a bright red sports car of course---a Porsche Boxer, such a 'guy' car, right...? I watched him pop out of it and grab his bags. He had several to my one, and I'm the girl, how funny. I watched the young man start to take them to the back of the plane as Collin handed him a tip.

His phone rang, and he stood at the base of the steps talking---very loudly too, as I could hear every word. The conversation was regarding the land deal in Sarasota tomorrow. They were going over transfer information for the closing. I find it weird to hear that he is a regular businessman doing real business. I just think of him as a killer. He said good bye to whomever and started up the steps. I was sitting there holding two glasses of champagne as he looked up.

"Well, look at you," he said with a smile.

"You got me at Florida---a free weekend of adventure. How could I say no to that," I said in playful tone.

"You won't regret it, the town has a nice little vibe going---it's known for its great food and art, art in all directions. Believe me, you will find some great and weird shit there, all mixed together."

"I'm looking forward to it, Collin, thank you for inviting me. Something I want understood, and I hope you respect my wishes. I don't want you to mention any of this to Toni, or anyone at the firm, ok?"

"Not a problem, I understand---our little secret, for now," he said as he sat with me and sipped his champagne. I watched out the window as we took off and made the turn over the Gulf of Mexico.

Chapter 22

Combined Chaos!

'Great things are done by a series of small things brought together.'

Vincent Van Gogh

"We can't lose this guy---move only if you can handle the cars too---they can't get away---any of them, Bobby."

"Done, Bobby out---John, car one, Tony, car two, Reese hit thug one, I'm on thug two---move, move..." said Bobby

"Chopper one, I have eyes on you, Bobby---we will grab anyone that may get clear---we've got your back."

Lizzy walked back to the bedroom and said, "I leave you boys alone for one minute and you have to find a fight to get into, really Jack?" laughed Lizzy.

"What you got, anything?"

"Ollie is looking now and I have him checking out of other states nearby as well---by the way, clean up at the Port is done. They have all the players at our team office in the city," said Lizzy.

"Hey Lizzy, text me Liam's number please?" asked Jack.

"When is the last time you talked to my ex, Jack?"

"Actually, last week. Bobby and I had a beer with him over at Mother's downtown," said Jack.

"How nice all you boys can be friends," Lizzy said with a sarcastic tone.

"Lizzy, just text me the number, thank you."

I didn't bother getting up, I just laid there and dialed the phone.

"Hello?"

"Hey, Liam, this is Jack, how's it going?"

"All good, we just got a call from Mississippi, a case, a Navy Lieutenant got herself raped and murdered in Biloxi, and the damn thing about it was she was hung upside down, like a cross..."

"Shit, don't move, Liam, we are on our way to you now---can you have everything from the scene ready – our cases just crossed buddy---this will be a one on the books visit, it seems. You're going to need to call your director, he is going to want to hear this," said Jack

"Ok, Jack, this sounds deep---anything to do with you shutting down the Port?" asked Liam.

"That's only part of it, we've got a shit storm here, and I can't trust locals or the Marshals. I even think our office may be infected.," said Jack.

"I understand, Jack, we will be ready for you at our new place." said Liam.

"See you there, Liam---are you at the Naval Air Station?" asked Jack.

"Yes, sir, new digs at JRB (Naval Air Station Joint Reserve Base). She has everything we need right at our fingertips."

Jack finds Lizzy in the bedroom half on a ladder and half on the swing bed looking at the ceiling with a flashlight.

"What in God's name are you doing up there?" yelled Jack.

"I found a couple of holes up here---did Domingo find any camera feeds when he was up here?" she asked.

"No, not when he swept the place, but I will ask him---come down we need to take a drive," said Jack.

"Where is this play-date going to take us to, Jack?"

He paused for a second then said, "JRB with Liam and his team," In the meantime, she climbed down from the ladder.

"That sounds just great, Liam, my ex. Why are we going to see him again? Lizzy whined.

"They just caught the Mississippi Murder, the jogger. She was Navy, Lizzy. We will need to brief his team on what we have and get them over to Mississippi. I actually called him to have his team look into that Mississippi Murder and keep us off the TV -– we are hot enough at the moment, with the Port and all. The victim just made this a joint effort with all their resources at our finger tips. Lizzy, we just caught another break,"Jack replied.

"Jack, this is a big break. We just bypassed any leaks we might face and can get some shit done now. Let me rub your forehead and catch some of that Jack luck going on…" Lizzy croaked, stupefied.

As Jack and Lizzy headed downstairs to the car, his phone buzzed, it was Liam – Jack flipped it open, "Hey Liam."

"Jack can you give the Director and I the short version, we need to read SEC-NAV in on this?"

"Ok Liam, here it comes---we are dealing with two different situations here and both seem to intersect with one another. On one hand we are looking for a sick display killer that killed a young woman, Sara, at Alligator Bayou. Who was under WITSEC protection, we know how that works. She is involved in some pretty strange stuff to begin with. We got a lead on a suspect from the Port.

Second, we are digging deep into an international human trafficking ring with something they call *The Factory. W*e believe it is a European baby factory set up for the specific use of the sex traffic trade. We can't trust the local P.D or the Marshals...

We have two of N.O.P.D.'s high ranking officers in custody---well, one is dead---for being part of it and we can't trust the Marshals due to some film we have. We think one of them may have had a relationship with the dead girl while she was in the WITSEC program. The ring seems to have its fingers into everyone down here. So, I need someone to trust, to help us with this. I've got to know the evidence is being processed right, Liam," Jack said as they sped through the French Quarter on their way to Liam's place.

Lizzy's phone started ringing. "Jack, its Ollie," she said."

Lizzy hit her ear piece to listen, and Jack picked up where he left off with Liam and the Director. "I know you'll have to get permission from our director, but please make sure *it's only him* you talk to---keep this as quiet as possible."

"Jack, this is Director Thompson. Not to worry, I'll call him personally for you, and Liam has my go ahead to give you all the support your team needs." said the Director.

"Thank you," said Jack with some relief.

"Jack---Jack, Ollie found bodies popping up all across the south and in Texas and Florida. Florida is leading the pack at this point," Lizzy said as she turned into the Base entrance.

"Hold on, Liam. Lizzy, what about his signature? The display, what about the display?"

"Jack, you're just going to be amazed at some of this shit---this is our guy! Domingo is sure and is sending us the files and photos, Jack---the number is at twenty nine so far..." said Lizzy with a bewildered look all over her face, as the base guard walked up to the car window.

"And we found nothing at the Port to connect him to the *Den*, right?" asked Jack.

"Nothing, you were right, except the teenager, she may have been an illegal trying to run from the mob. So they are not connected in any way as far as we can tell, except through Sara, Jack."

"I'm asking about the other kills and does the signature in those cases match, do they match up with our guy's pattern?" asked Jack in a stern tone.

"Yes, you can see that when he started, he wasn't as developed as he is now, but the crude signature is evident, Jack. We are waiting on the photo gallery Domingo put together for us. Give me just a minute and let's get in the Base, then I will throw it up on the wall for us, ok?" said Lizzy.

The guard asked for ID as they both sat there, "Excuse me, I need to see your ID's!" The guard snapped in a sharp tone. We flipped our badges for the guard, he raised his hand and motioned for the gate to be raised.

Chapter 23

Flash Drive

'Wit as an instrument of revenge is as infamous as art is as a means of sensual titillation.'

Karl Wilhelm & Fredrich Schiegel

The pilot came over the intercom asking us to buckle up for landing as we circled the city of Sarasota. A couple of minutes later, the wheels squealed and we were on the ground. Just ahead of the jet was a beautiful white Bentley convertible rolling up to meet us.

Now remember, this was my first time away with him, so I didn't really know if this was his norm or if he was putting on a show for me. Either way, I was enjoying it. I already made up my mind I was going to stay in costume while here. I didn't want anything to lead back to me later.

 Thinking about it, I needed to give Jack a call, just to keep things going and have him still thinking I was in Europe.

We reached the Westin, the new hotel deal Collin put together some time ago. Tonight was the grand opening, and a Millionaire's Ball was taking place in the Triton Ballroom. Then, there was an auction at the rooftop bar, where some of the local affluent men and women would be sold to the highest bidders for a night of private fun, which sounded right up his twisted alley, right...?

Collin had arranged for me to have my own room, and it was on the top floor overlooking both the city and the Bay. This place was so clean and fresh looking, but not very homie, very static looking. The view was nice, but my city was better. He also had a black evening gown laid across my bed with all the fixings---shoes, jewelry and of course some sexy lingerie complete with a garter belt and white stockings---such a guy thing to do... But he does have great taste.

I'm planning on wearing my favorite black shag cut wig with white face makeup---not totally Goth, but close enough to stand out and make them remember I was there, for sure. And still be an invisible woman to them all.

Collin wasn't expecting me downstairs until six. That gave me time to take a bath and think a little, about how to play this guy and keep things moving forward. I didn't want him to get suspicious, because this could go bad for me in a hurry! I began to drop my cloths to the floor. I stood in front of the full-length mirror naked, and realized that tonight this killer, the man that killed my sister, would try to kiss me.

The thought of that just sent me to the cold tile floor, throwing up in the toilet. How could I let his lips touch mine after knowing what he had done? I eased myself back on the cold tile and laid there watching the fan spin around and around. Images of his face coming at me and his hands on my shoulders made me sit up dry heaving and choking again.

I had to get over this, but how, knowing what I know. I can't just close my eyes and let it happen---I will throw up in his mouth... That made me laugh, I needed that. I was able to get up and crawl in the tub of hot steamy water.

I sank down in the water and closed my eyes, which didn't help---due to the thoughts and visions of him and Sara that just kept flooding my mind.

I kept telling myself that this was the right thing to do, and he needed to pay for all the bad he had done---to feel the same pain he liked to dish out. I just needed to find a way to walk through this.

After I was done being mind-fucked, I walked out into the bedroom and sat near the window and looked at the dress and lingerie. The bewitching hour was almost here.

The hotel phone rang, and I walked over to the desk in front of the window and answered it---it was him. "Yes, how can I help you, sir?" I said in a playful tone.

His reply was classic, "I have a couple of great ideas we can share later."

I just stared at my naked reflection in the glass of the window, and answered with a sexy, "Well then, sir, it sounds like a yummy evening ahead." Fighting back the chokes of vomit racing up my throat, as I fell forward against the glass window. He gave a chuckle, and said he would see me in the lobby...

I walked over to the glass doors that led out to the balcony and flung them open and made my way out to the open. I stood there with my face to the sky, not caring that I was naked and exposed. I needed answers and quick. My date with a killer was here. Then all the words Jean had said the other night at dinner came rushing in and the feeling took my body over. I was the Queen of New Orleans, and this piece of shit was of no value to anyone, except to be dead.

I walked into the bedroom and began to dress. My hands felt like silk as the stockings slid up my legs. I actually thought about not wearing the panties---and I thought, this is my show, so, no panties tonight. The dress fit like a perfectly fitted glove, taking advantage of every curve and giving it the attention it deserved. The white make-up almost matched my milky white skin to complete tonight's display of total desire in black heels.

I headed for the door and saw a nice pure silver letter opener sitting on the hall table next to my black gloves---my black gloves with a surprise sewn inside them. I picked it up and held it up to the light and said, "Hell, tonight might be the night for all this to end." I lifted my dress and began to ease it into the top of my stocking, the cold metal touched my skin and I about had an orgasm standing there in the doorway. What kind of shit is all this…

I slipped on my gloves and walked to the elevator and went down to the lobby to find Mr. Murder Man and start this game, but, the game was going to be played *my* way. I was the bitch in control. The doors opened, and I walked out into the unknown of the evening. A waiter stood there with a tray of Champagne. I reached for a glass and told the waiter to stay in my sight and keep my glass full at all times. I blew him a kiss, and licked my lips, just for giggles… I thought this guy was going to drop the tray, how funny.

In the distance I saw him. He was talking it up with three delicious other men, as if they jumped out of a catalog of the new hipster vibe guy or whatever. I made my way to them, and stood about three steps from them, just sipping my champagne. My little man was standing to my left, ready to pour too. The three delicious treats turned, and eye fucked me as I stood there. I stepped forward and lifted my fingers to one of their mouths and shut it for him. Collin leaned in and kissed my cheek.

I smiled and said, "Hello, boys."

Collin lifted my arm and escorted me into the Ball and onto the dance floor. We danced forever. I could see Collin getting himself all worked up for what he thought was going to be a good evening. The poor boy is in for one hell of confusing disappointment that he just won't remember. I whispered in his ear that we needed a drink and some cool air. Collin spun me off the floor and right up to a waiter holding a tray of yummy champagne. I grabbed one off the tray and took it all in one swallow.

Collin stood there, sipping slowly as he smiled, but his eyes were empty, with pure evil pouring out. I knew he was planning what he was going to do to me in the wee hours of the coming morning. Unfortunately, he was coming too late to that party… I had the first strike already planned for his ass. I turned and walked to the elevator and stood with my back to him and the entire room, though I could see everything through the reflection on the elevator doors.

The doors opened, and I stepped in and turned placing both hands on the steel railing, what a picture that was. Collin couldn't help but jump on before the doors shut and sent me away without him. He stood in front of me almost waiting for permission to kiss me. This was a stone cold serial killer, groveling at my finger-tips---who would of thought. The strangest thing began to happen on our ride up to the rooftop club. I could see faces of all the women, the women he had played with and killed over the years.

They filled this small box, it filled up fast, I eased my hand to the cold silver tucked in my stockings and began to pull it out and plant it deep in his heart---when the doors opened, and night air flooded in with jazzy music and people talking loudly. That killed the mood, if you know what I mean. We stepped out and he made his way over to the bar to get us a couple of drinks. I walked right down the middle of the room and dance floor, with not a care in the world. I ended at the rail overlooking this cute city.

Collin found me and handed me my drink, with a smile and an evil wink--- *do you really think I'm dumb enough to drink this shit?* It would be the last cocktail of my life if I did, so I pulled the old slip off my high heel trick and dropped my drink of death over the railing, save… I watched his face distort itself in horror as his plan just got kicked in the nuts. I grabbed his arm and I did my fake fall. He helped me up and I quickly blew the white powder into his face that I had waiting in the palm of my glove. He threw his head back and wiped his face, but it was too late. I heard him sniff twice, and knew he was mine.

His face was red, and those evil eyes began to glaze over with total submission. I began to call his name, "Collin, Collin, are you ok, sweetie?"

As I rolled my gloves off very carefully and dropped them in the trash barrel as I guided him to the elevator, I pushed the button, but the door didn't open right away. He had this drunken look, while being very awake. Collin started to move to the music, and I actually joined in, after all, he's my play toy now---anything I want, he will do and never remember. This is a great dress rehearsal for Savannah.

The doors opened, and we danced in. I pushed him up against the side wall and pushed lobby, then asked him if he had been a bad boy lately.

"I am a real bad boy. I have lots of secrets that no one knows about," Collin said with a smile and a lost gaze in his eyes.

I leaned in and whispered in his ear, "Tell me how bad you have been, Collin? Tell me your secrets, Collin."

"I'm a naughty, naughty boy. I like to hurt weak girls and then display them like my prizes for everyone to see how powerful I am."

"Collin, why do you do all those naughty things to all those girls?' I asked.

He began to roll his head and squirm around the elevator as if he were trying to climb the walls. As he began to answer, my hand was gripped around the cold silver opener in the back of my stockings once again.

"I like it, well, I get a little edgy before business deals, and it gives me such a release and then such a rush, which helps me to focus---so I need it and who doesn't need a little *get off.*" The ding of the elevator bell broke my interrogation. We stepped out, well I stepped---Collin kind of fell out. I had to help him walk down the hall to his room across from mine, where I opened his door and ordered him to walk over to the bed and start to undress. He staggered over and fell forward onto the king bed laughing.

He finally stood up throwing his shirt to the right and his pants to the left. I then told him to slip his briefs down and to jack himself off on the bed.

Without blinking, he went to work. I took this time to place my clothes around the room to make it look like I was playing along too. As he groaned, I knew he was done and I told him to stand there and wait for my next command. Collin did just that---stood there like a nice boy.

I finished staging the room with all my clothes and walked over to the desk and sat in the leather chair. The leather was cold against my naked butt, it was nice for a second. I flipped open his laptop and ordered him to tell me the password---he just stood there weaving back and forth not saying a word. I jumped out of the chair and walked over to him. Collin had his eyes closed and was making this buzzing sound.

I slapped his face and told him to tell me the password. Still nothing, just buzzing and weaving. Do I risk more Devils breath? Well, on the down side it will kill him, and I go home, or it does what I want, and I get the password and get the information on all that he has done. Either way I'm good, right…?

Chapter 24

New Discoveries!

'The real voyage of discovery consists not in seeking new landscapes, but in having new eyes.'

Marcel Proust

Jack and Lizzy pulled up to Liam's office next to the helicopter field. Liam was standing outside ready to greet them.

"Liam, good to see you and thank you again for all this. We really need some good eyes on this case. How fast can you get you and your team up to speed on this and take a look at what we have collected so far?" I asked.

"Jack, I had my guys wired in on the conversation we had on the way in, so they are well on their way now---I had Domingo hook up with Tommy, when he gets back on the Base. Then we can be in the air on a moment's notice. Mississippi is the latest kill for our guy, right?"

"It looks like Mississippi has that honor, Liam."

"The jogger, the Naval Officer down by the Gulf, she was hung upside down on the bridge overpass---like an upside-down cross, right?" said Liam.

"Yes, that's her. Our guy displays his victims in an elaborate way---we have dubbed him the Sacrifice Killer. That title, by the way, is just for us, not the public, ok?" said Jack.

Liam pointed to the door, as they made their way inside to talk. "Jack, I understand completely. We will keep this quiet for you, my team knows better anyway... My team left ten minutes ago for the site in Biloxi, but we have them on live feed over here for the sit-rep Jack."

"Well then, look who is cutting to the chase now, brother---you Navy boys are on top of the game," laughed Jack

"But it takes us Navy girls to kick them into shape, agent Bode'," Mindy, Liam's right hand, barked back at Jack over the screen.

"Sorry Mindy, I didn't mean anything. The story is, the FBI---is short people and we asked NCIS for crime scene help---we keep it at that and hopefully there will be no questions. Who is running your Forensics lab?" asked Jack.

"Tory is still there, you remember her, right? Didn't you and she...?"

Jack sat there with a sheepish grin on his face, knowing full well, him and Tory had a great summer two years ago, before she left for Iraq.

His only response was, "Oh, really."

Liam just laughed and told the helicopter pilot to land the team on the other side of the road away from the murder scene. The press had already set up camp on the hillside near the hotel---they were able to get some great shots from that angle.

Liam's team had set up a tent over the victim to get a little privacy, and some shade from the boiling Mississippi sun. Tommy was wearing a body-cam so the team back home could be part of every move on the ground. Tommy entered the tent giving everyone a close-up of the body. Without looking their way, Tory said "Hi, Jack, stop staring at my ass---it's been awhile---doing ok, are you?" as she pulled the girl's tongue out.

Both Jack and Liam about lost it---the poor girl had been hanging there for a good bit of time now. She was a little ripe. Tory laughed and told the boys to look at what she had found under the tongue. That caught their attention pretty quick---a piece of Velcro, like from a ball gag under the tip of the tongue. Jack asked if there were any other marks. Tory said nothing she could find.

"I would like to see any other victims you have to compare the details we can't see yet." Tory said as she pulled off her gloves and told the two techs to cut her down and bag her.

"Lizzy, we need Tory to take a look at---oh shit, never mind---we don't have her body. Did we get any detailed photos before she went up in flames?" Jack asked.

"Yes, Jack, the lab in Baton Rouge has them. I will have them sent over to Tory now. I also have Ollie sending the names of the other girls that may be part of this guy's kill list---we could possibly pull them up for review." Lizzy said without even looking at the boys, as she pecked away on the keyboard.

"Jack, she hasn't changed a bit, has she?

"No, Lizzy has always been one step ahead of us, every time, Liam. She has always been a great asset. She has always had that great sense about things."

After Tory zipped up the body bag and sent it on its way to the air base, she stood in front of the camera and told the team she found three numbers carved into the girl's neck just under the back of her hair. Jack leaned in and kissed the screen as he ran out to call Ollie, with Liam right behind him. Tory yelled into the screen, but it was too late---he was gone.

"For Christ sake---somebody tell him I read a report a week ago about a girl from Georgia with the same carving and numbers," Tory exclaimed.

 Tommy grabbed his mike, "Liam, Tory found a link between bodies, but we don't know how it fits in yet---this guy is cutting the numbers 389 on the backside of his victim's necks, do you copy?"

Liam looked over Jack's way and said, "Jack, have you seen anything like this before, is this a double signature?"

"What are you talking about Liam, Double Signature?" Jack stood there with the phone in his hand looking dumbfounded.

"Sorry, I thought you were wired in with us---Tommy just clicked in---Tory read a report a week back about a girl in Georgia, same cuts, same numbers---we have a link!"

"Ok, the numbers mean something to him, more personal than ego-driven, like the displays---that's ego, the numbers, that's personal," Jack implied.

"I can see that, Jack, can you break this guy down for me---I mean your version of him, Jack, not the profile?" Liam asked.

"Well at first, we saw Sara hanging in this tree, like we have never seen before. Super elaborate, hang-men's knot---the way she was laid out. We thought this might be related to the Romanians and their weird shit. Now remember, the DNA from the cabin turned out to be from Garner, the Romanian, but that's where it didn't fit for me. They needed her. I'm sorry, they both needed her---the Mob and the Marshals. Then we began to see the pattern of kills throughout the South---yes, that still fits with the Mob---but not really.

The Mob had no reason to kill her, Sara had her own insurance policy, so to speak, and the Idiot Marshal had fallen for her. Sara was feeding Justice with all the information they needed to take down an international sex ring, with a baby factory in Europe, from what we have been told. We are still putting all those pieces together by the way. But as for the focus changing, Lizzy and Ollie found a string of murders with the display signature all over them---some of the earliest ones were a bit crude though, that started as far back as the eighties, but his signature was there and developing.

Liam, this guy is very intelligent, organized, and has money. I'm going to say he is a good-looking guy---with game, to be able to lure these women. Remember, they aren't prostitutes. Look at the jogger and the victim from upstate. Tory said she was a Lawyer, and Sara wasn't an outright hooker, she was a Dominatrix, a super shape girl by everything we can tell.

We don't know how he picks them yet, or if he does any research on them. They may just be random victims, victims of opportunity for all we know. This has been going on for years, for God's sake, with no end in sight unless we catch a break soon."

Jack's phone rang with an overseas number, "Hello, this is agent Bode'."

"Hey, Jack" Raven said in a slow weak tone.

"Raven, are you ok, is everything alright?"

"Yes, Jack, I'm fine, I wanted to call and see how things are going---did you get him yet?"

"No, we are getting closer though, my team is hard at it as we speak."

"Can you tell me anything, what do you have?"

"I'm sorry, Raven, I can't, I hope you understand?"

"Sure, I will talk to you soon then." Buzz, then the line went dead.

Jack just stood and looked out onto the runway. Liam walked back inside to the team as Lizzy asked where Jack was. Liam told her he was outside on the phone with a Raven...

"Who is Raven?" Liam asked

"She is the dead girl's sister, that Jack has taken a shining to, if you know what I mean," Lizzy explained.

"Why is this the first we are hearing of her---she was the victim's sister?"

"She is in Europe mourning the death of Sara, Liam."

"And" Liam exclaimed, "has she been cleared or even talked to about all this?"

"Started to, but that's when the lightning hit the tree and the body, and evidence went up in flames. She drove off in her sister's car and we haven't seen her since."

"Really, Lizzy?"

"Yep, that's it, everything went up in flames. He didn't tell you that part?"

"No, he left that out, it seems."

Jack walked back into the briefing room with all eyes on him. "What, do I have a booger on my face?"

Liam looked at him and said, "As a matter of fact you do, in a manner of speaking. Did you want to tell me about the tree and body at the Bayou? And the sister you have no idea of where she is?"

As Jack looked around the room, he was a loss for words at that moment, and he didn't even try to answer the questions. Jack just threw his hands in the air and said, "Well, shit."

Jack's phone rang, breaking the tension in the room. It was Bobby with details on the event at the cabin back at Alligator Bayou,

"Jack, we just set up---we don't have anything yet---but I think I may have found a little tweety bird, Jack…"

Chapter 25

Let's Play!

'When she's abandoned her moral center and teachings… when she's cast aside her façade of propriety and lady-like demeanor… when I have so corrupted this fragile thing and brought out a writhing, mewling, bucking, wanton whore for my enjoyment and pleasure… enticing from within this feral lioness… growling and scratching and biting… taking everything I dish out to her… at that moment she is never more beautiful to me.

Marquis de Sade

I walked over to my purse to get the small vial of devil's breath, when Collin's phone rang My eyes shot over to where he was standing---he wasn't in this world, lucky for me… On my way back to the bed I grabbed a spoon from the tray on the desk. I jumped up on the bed and stepped over to him straddling his head and while I gently poured the white powder into the spoon and asked Collin to look up.

He slowly raised his head, letting his blood shot evil eyes look into mine when I blew. He sniffed and grabbed his head before falling at my feet on the bed. He stopped the buzzing and replaced it with a low moan. I gave it a second, then asked him to look at me now standing naked over him on the bed.

"Collin, what is your secret password baby, tell me your secret."

"Mommy389."

"I'm sure that means something, tell me why you use that, Collin," I said as I squatted closer to his face.

"My mom was a street whore on heroin. My father used to make me watch as he had his way with her and other women. He would shoot them up and then do all those things to them."

"Did he kill them?" I asked with a quiver in my tone.

"No, he was too weak for that shit---that was me, all me---I did the killing of the whores and I liked it very much."

"Collin, how old were you when you started?"

"Maybe ten, maybe, it was mom. She was my first…Dad didn't touch another girl for a long time after that."

I fell over right onto the floor as those words left his mouth. I didn't expect that. What happened to him to make him kill his mother, for God's sake. Can someone be born this way?

I pulled myself up off the floor and poured myself a drink, straight Bourbon---I took it all with one gulp---how could I not. At that moment I wanted to tie him up, but that wouldn't work in the plan. What is a girl to do…?

"Collin, call your pilot and have him ready for a flight to Savannah in the morning. You're taking me to see the city!"

"Ok, Savannah, see the city."

Collin said good-bye as I took the phone from his ear. I walked over to the desk and sat with Collin's laptop in my lap, so I could keep an eye on the monster. The password worked, boy did it work---files just started popping up, all with a different picture of a woman as file covers, within a couple of seconds the screen was full of women, lost women, dead women. I fumbled for the flash drive stick thing I laid on the desk. It took me a second to get it in, my hands were shaking from what I was seeing.

These files were organized by the girl's first name and the state he killed her in. My God, the list of states!---Louisiana, Texas, Florida, South Carolina, North Carolina, Georgia, Alabama, and Mississippi---each state had multiple layers of files stacked up. Some stacks as many as ten-deep.

I took a second to prepare before I clicked into one of them, but I did click and closed my eyes as I pushed the button. Then realizing I couldn't see the monster on the bed with my eyes closed, I quickly opened them to horrifying images on the screen. I lost my cookies right there in the chair and blessed the floor with a puddle of vomit…

I was able to lock focus on the face of the woman in the pictures, the pain, and the terror in her eyes. I could almost feel what she was going through, what Sara must have gone through. I just wanted to walk over and thrust the letter opener into his forehead and kill the bastard and end this now. Then a blip on the screen with a box popped up and read 'download complete'.

I stood and placed the laptop back on the desk, wiped the search history and cleared the cookies, everything my computer guy back home taught me. I even wiped it down with a wash cloth for safety measures, after all it had been on my naked lap… I looked around to see if I had missed anything before I took a shower to try to wash this evil off me. I grabbed my letter opener and locked the bathroom door behind me, the shower was a fast one, not very relaxing, I'll tell you, but it helped…

I dressed and stood in the bathroom door towel drying my hair as Collin began to stir in the bed. He was still naked, and I'll bet he woke up with one hell of a headache. I watched him as he made little groan noises and rolled around. He finally stood up and walked over and kissed me on the cheek and said he was taking a shower. I smiled and closed the bathroom door. I went immediately to his laptop and opened it again, just to double check I had got out clean. I called Jean-Paul to make sure he had Savannah set up for me.

He asked if I was really ok with what I was about to do. He told me that he would be glad to do it for me, and that I could watch as he used his special gifts on the dirt bag. I must say that did sound very interesting to me, but I knew inside I had to be the one. The hotel phone rang. Collin popped his head out of the bathroom with a puzzled look, and I shrugged my shoulders as I picked it up and said good morning---

"Good morning, ma'am this is the front desk, your car is here to take you to the airport."

"Ok, thank you---we will be down in a minute." I said with a happy tone and shot a smile Collin's way, for added cover on my evil little plan. We will see if the Devils Breath really works in about a second…

"Why are they calling? Why are we leaving so soon?" quizzed Collin, as he made his way into the room and started getting dressed.

"Collin, we are going to Savannah. The Southern Night's Jubilee you raved about last night, after you had your way with me, remember?" He stood there, and you could tell he was searching his brain for the answer; now his ego should kick in.

I needed to throw him a bone and keep him off kilter, "Catch these." as I threw him my black panties from last night.

His face lit up and he smiled at me, but his eyes told a different story---his brain was telling him he fucked me last night, but he couldn't remember anything. I undid my pants and opened them just enough for him to see my purple panties, and I said, "These are for tonight---ready to go yet…"

He began to fumble for his clothes, and pack, all at the same time. This is a great feeling, let me tell you. Control over a killer like Collin. A knock at the door broke the tension in the room. A voice called out, "Bellboy, ma'am." I walked over to the door and let him in as Collin zipped up and threw the guy his bag. Then we made our way out the door to the elevator.

Collin opened his phone and called his pilot, "James, I need the plane ready for a flight to Savannah in about thirty minutes."

"Sir, you called me last night, we are ready for you now, wheels up!"

Collin held the phone to his ear, but you could hear the silence of nothing there. I could see he didn't like the not knowing, and the lack of control over the events un-folding before him. He had been in total control of every aspect of everything…now he couldn't remember last night, any detail about last night or today---he is a killer in the dark and I hold the light switch now.

Chapter 26

Gypsy Summer

'Knowledge is power. Information is power. The secreting or hoarding of knowledge or information may be an act of tyranny camouflaged as humility.'

Robin Morgan

Seven quiet pops filled the foggy night air at Alligator Bayou. Seven men fell to the black muck. Bobby gave the order to move in. The team moved in from out of the shadows of the Bayou, converging on the open spot in front of the cabin area. Each team member now standing over their target's body.

Henry was still on his knees in the center of the circle of dead men, his hands in the air, shaking like he had a bad case of Parkinson's. He kept repeating in Cajun, "Don't kill me, don't kill me…" The boys had their red lasers dancing all over Henry. I think he peed his pants as well.

Bobby motioned for the team to grab ID's of the dead men and get them out of sight, as he grabbed Henry and started to drag him to the cabin. Inside, Bobby slammed him in a chair and began zip tying him to that chair. Once the men finished cleaning up the mess, they unloaded Colter from the truck and met Bobby in the cabin.

"Put him up on the ladder and hook the generator up outside the kitchen door, and gentlemen, put the bag of tools on that end of the table. Let's make sure he is double-zip-tied---this is going to hurt," smiled Bobby.

Henry pulled against his zip ties as he watched from the chair Bobby had tied him to. Roscoe pushed his ear mic and gave orders to the two men hooking up the generator.

"Hey, guys, stay on the perimeter---be like shadows and sink their cars in the Bayou. No comes one in and no one goes out, copy?"

"Check."

Bobby called Evan over and told him to hike up to Henry's place and find anything and everything. Evan, the youngest of the team, had a nose for the unusual hiding places and the things that are out of place. They call him the bloodhound, and they know he will always find something. Bobby walked over to the bag on the table and rolled it out; knives, hammers, picks, saws, and a hand drill came into view.

Colter didn't even flinch, but Henry on the other hand started squirming and mumbling. Bobby asked if he would like to go first---as Bobby squeezed the trigger to the hand drill. This action sent a high pitched whining sound throughout the cabin. Colter just started laughing, like this was all a big joke.

The kitchen door cracked open, and two men outside stepped in to let Bobby know the generator was up and ready.

"Thank you, guys. Hit the perimeter and stay out of sight. Now for you, Henry, would you like the drill or the battery cables?" Bobby reached under the table and came up with the red and black handles of some very heavy-duty battery cables. With both hands he struck them together, throwing sparks and flashes all around the cabin.

"Man, this will hurt. Let me show you, Henry." Bobby leaned in as he began to rub the ends together as yellow sparks flew all over Henry.

"No, hell no, mister. I love the money, but I love my life better."

At that moment Colter looked down at Henry from the ladder he was strapped to, and said, "Go ahead old man talk and see what you get, *ta mort*."

Bobby reached up to his right and rested the cable handles on Colter's ankle lighting him up like a bobble head on crack. His head twisted, and drool dripped out of his mouth as his eyes rolled back into his head.

"Well, it's nap time for him. Now for you, Henry?"

"I'm good, sir. Where do you want me to start the story, and you can tell your guy to look behind my chair in the living room for all the photos and my record book."

"That's a great start, Henry. So, the *Den*---how does it work?"

Henry cleared his throat and began to explain that, back in the mid-sixties, a group of folks came to stay at the cabins. It was a summer of gypsies. It turned out they were real gypsies, too. They all had children with them, girls, each couple had two young girls with them and they all seemed to know each other. He meant the parents were the ones that knew each other--- not the kids---because before long, Henry noticed each year it would be the same people, but different girls.

Then about two summers in, the gypsies noticed Henry was catching on to something going on with the children, because one morning a black car showed up at his cabin. It was filled with men in black suits, each man had a gun tucked into his belt. They asked if he would come with them, to have some chicory with their boss. He didn't think he would have lived much past that morning, if he had said no.

Bobby said, "Jack, remember this was back in the sixties---that far back."

"I got that Bobby, go on."

Then Henry went on to say, the car took him to the Port, the same Port we just locked down. He told us they pulled up to a large ship that was docked near the end of the Port. It was unloading those multi-colored metal containers. They walked onto that ship, and they led him to the rear of the giant ship, and up some metal steps to a wide metal plank with a wall of containers (as he put it). Two of them that were towards the middle of the wall were open, with a view out onto the Mississippi. He could hear music and people talking as they got closer.

"Jack, Henry began to describe the inside of the metal boxes. He told us that they were set up like city apartments, but with a better view---that's for sure. Henry said these were like what he had seen in New Orleans years earlier---they had sofas, a table and chairs, a bar, even beds towards the back of them. They had power and lights up and down the inside of these containers. Henry also told us that there were young women all over the place giving men drinks and doing other stuff right there in the open. He said he was very embarrassed and didn't want to look.

Jack, this may have been a time of free love and all, but this was anything but free--- Henry fell right in the middle of the *Den*. Henry told us, as they sat him down at a table near the water, he could see steps, spiral steps that led up to the container above the ones he was sitting at. The men from the car stood next to him until a man walked out, a man dressed in what Henry described as a red robe, but he said the man was dressed very nice under it---like a businessman.

The man sat and took a sip of his chicory coffee as he looked out onto the Mississippi. A young girl walked over and whispered in his ear, which made the man laugh and clap his hands, then at that moment turned and looked at Henry. No words just an ominous look. The man motioned for Henry to drink. Henry said he thanked the man, but said no. The man looked over at a young girl and waved her over. She stood in front of Henry, that's when the man spoke for the first time. He spoke in a broken English talk, as Henry put it. He said maybe Russian, but he was no judge."

"Henry, you have hurt my feelings. I want to share a cup of coffee with you, but you refuse me. This is not a good way to start our relationship, Henry. My people tell me they like your cabins very much. They tell me you are a very good host, but you may be getting a little funny about their business, my business. Is this true, my friend?"

Henry looked up and said, "I don't understand the different children every year--- that's all, sir?"

"Jack, that's not how I would have started the conversation if it had been me. You know what I'm saying, but hey, he is still alive. "

He went on to say, the man said, "Henry, we operate an adoption service for our special clients with special needs. We have been doing this for many years – we find places to meet and exchange the children. Then my people deliver the children to their new families, see---simple. Your Bayou is just one of hundreds of places across America we do this, and we have double that amount in Europe. We even have a *factory* there as well."

"Ok, sir. I think I understand."

"Henry, being a man of few words, didn't really know how to mix it up with people like this. Maybe, that's why this guy likes him, and he is still alive, Jack."

Henry said the man went on to say, "Well, Henry, I don't think you really do understand---we need to make sure you do because my business is very important to me---these girls are very special to me. So, you see, Henry, we are going to have to make sure you really do understand."

Henry said the man began to speak in his talk to the girls, and the one standing in front of him dropped her clothes, then sat down on Henry's lap, and began to kiss his cheek as a guard started taking pictures. Henry sat there stunned.

"Now, Henry, wasn't that fun, so we are friends, no…?"

The man pointed to the girl and she hopped off his lap and began to pick up her clothes, and then she disappeared into the container.

The man slid a stack of money, a lot of money, over to Henry and said, "Henry, I like my friends and take good care of my friends---see, Henry, you will get one of these each time my families come and stay in your cabins---ok? Or do you just want me to shoot you now and have my guys throw you into the Mississippi. Henry, that would make me sad, I like you."

Henry said he looked over at the man, and in a bold tone told him, "All you had to do, sir, was shake my hand. I would have been fine with that---all this other shit was not needed, mister, not needed, sir."

Henry said the man sat there looking out at the Mississippi, reached for a cigar and lit it and took two puffs then turned to Henry and said, "Henry, you are right, I get carried away sometimes. I'm passionate about my girls."

The man stood and held out his hand and said, "Henry, my friend, my name is *Regele*, that means *The King*."

"Jack, after that, Henry looked me right in the eyes and said these words, "Get yourself ready, lawman. This is only the beginning of some wild gypsy shit…"

Chapter 27

Mirror, Mirror

'Mirror, Mirror on the wall, tell me something, tell me who's the loneliest of all? Fear of what's inside of me; tell me, can a heart be turned to stone? Mirror, mirror, what's behind you? Save me from the things I see! I can keep it from the world, why won't you let me hide from me? Mirror, mirror, tell me something, who's the loneliest of all? I'm the loneliest of all.'

Jeff Williams

The jet made its turn north for a path to Savannah, Georgia. Collin looked a little off center with the chain of events over the past twenty-four hours. This guy has just lost his edge, and he can't seem to get control back... I sat next to him and kissed him, told him how great he was last night and that I was hoping for some of the same tonight.

I reached down between his legs and gave him a squeeze before getting up and getting a glass of champagne. "Collin, would you like a glass?"

He smiled and gave me a half nod. I poured our glasses, slipping a little something extra in his as I gave it a swirl... I handed it to him as I sat down again, Collin toppled the glass then set it on the table. I gently stroked his forehead as he drifted into a sleep. This should last until we landed---I had to hope anyway. I went to the back of the jet and called Jean to make sure his people were ready on the ground.

They were to have a driver and a Bentley at the gate with reservations set up at the Westin in Collin's name. Jean-Paul assured me everything would be as I directed, and back-up would be ready if needed. He reminded me to stay out of sight, public view, and not to use any credit cards. I told him I was wearing my red wig and black leather. He laughed and told me that would work in the city of ghosts...

The Pilot announced that we were on approach and would be on the ground in five minutes. I could see Collin stir in his seat, so I said good bye to Jean and rushed back to my seat to keep Collin confused. This cat and mouse game is kind of cool. It's funny, I have to make this shit up on the fly, then work it into my overall plan---maybe I am really good at this shit, as Jean-Paul keeps telling me.

The jet wheels hit the tarmac with a bounce and a screech---Savannah, the future resting place of Collin Strapmore. Collin was a prolific serial killer, to put it mildly, who the FBI had no idea about but have dubbed him *'The Sacrifice Killer',* due to how this guy displayed his victims, which included my sister Sara. Well, I now hold all his files and photos of his 1,228 victims, innocent young women that for no reason got in his way and his sickness took over.

Tomorrow this chapter, as fun and revealing as it turned out to be, will come to a close. My life can get back to normal, even though I might not know what normal means anymore---if you know what I mean. I am going to have to take a couple of days to get my head back on track before heading back to the Big O, and I know where I want to go to do that--- Charleston by the ocean, to sip some wine and watch waves.

A shot of air sounded and the door to the jet lowered. The pilot entered and asked how the flight was? I told him it was heavenly. Collin woke up to us talking, and he stretched his arms like he was ready to go.

He looked out the window and asked, "Where are we again?"

The pilot told him we were in Savannah, Georgia, with a temperature of a balmy 82 degrees.

Collin looked up at me and asked, "Why did we come here to begin with?"

"Collin, you remember right?"

"No, I don't."

"Well, last night as I was on top of you, you told me you were taking me to Savannah for some Festival---that this place was special to you---The Westin and all, that this was all about me…"

Collin was again taken by surprise and showed it, something he is not used to. He began to fumble around and search for words, "Yes, yes, anything for you, this weekend is all for you, Raven." You could tell he had to struggle with those words. A beep sounded, breaking the moment. We turned to see a five-foot man standing in the doorway. He tipped his hat and said, "Good day, my name is Brazil, I'm your driver." He smiled up at me, his teeth glimmering against his black skin. Raven knew she didn't have a thing to worry about.

The Pilot said he would show him where the bags were, as we grabbed our things and headed to the car. Collin opened my door and helped me in, then stepped away from the car and made a call. I wanted to know what he was up to really bad, but couldn't do a thing. I felt a little helpless. No sooner than a blink, Collin joined me in the car and I asked if everything was ok.

He answered me with, "Funny, I don't remember calling my office and changing my schedule. This whole thing is strange," as he held the phone and looked at it. I told him he had called them last night after we had our sweaty, sticky fun, and that he was very excited about it.

Then I turned to him and said, "Collin, thank you for this. I can't wait for tomorrow and the picnic and bike ride."

"Bike ride, I don't ride bikes," he said with his shoulders held back as the car sped off to the hotel. I noticed Brazil watching in the mirror, he smiled and winked back at me. I explained to Collin that he had agreed to go to Cock-Spur Island and have a picnic while riding bikes. I leaned in and began to whisper in his ear, that if he would think about the little fantasy I shared with him, he would be a very happy boy tomorrow.

His face froze as he searched his brain for the words I had shared with him last night, but the thing is… I never really said a thing, but he doesn't know that, how fun is this, right? The Devil's Breath is some great shit…

"Collin, swinging from the tree overlooking the river, remember…?" I watched as his eyes narrowed and a smile came over him. You see I just planted a familiar vision in his killer head and that will be hard for him to resist. I have to keep his head twisted up, so he stays off balance for me.

The honk of the car's horn snapped both of us to the valet holding the door for us to get out and head up our room. I stepped out with my head down, as I put on my floppy hat and stopped at the curb to look for something I didn't really need, as they made their way into the hotel. As Brazil looked back over his shoulder as they disappeared in the hotel, I walked over to the side entrance and slipped in that way.

I could hear kids making pool noises just ahead. I would be safe there, until he checked in and wondered where I have gotten off to. Besides, I already knew what room and Brazil slipped me a key, so I'm good. Jean-Paul made sure it was a suite at the end of the hall right next to the stairway for added get-a-way effect. The head of security is an old family friend of his, so there will be no video of me while I'm here.

I finally wandered up to the room, and found the door open. Collin was out on the balcony talking on the phone. I poured two glasses of wine and walked out to him, handed him a glass, while listening to his conversation. It was something about land in the south part of Savannah about ten minutes from the hotel. I walked to the doorway and stopped, with my back to him dropping my dress and walked into the bathroom---I heard him say, "I've got to go."

I shut the door behind me and locked it, made sure it was locked before getting into the shower. I did yell out to him to order dinner. I wanted room service and his attention tonight. All I heard was, "On it…" I showered, but I really didn't want to go back out there. I had no idea what to expect, see, this is the part of the plan that has to be ad-libbed. I had no way of knowing what was going to happen from minute to minute.

I toweled off then wrapped myself in it and grabbed the handle of the door with one hand and the handle of my letter opener with my other, just in case. I peeked through the crack of the door and saw him sitting on the sofa reading something on his computer. He had no idea I was there, which was good for me. I slipped into the hotel robe and my panties, not really having a place for my trusty letter opener. So, I snapped it in the edge of my panties and hoped for the best.

I walked back into the bathroom and grabbed my little round blush container, which was holding my Devil's Breath for me. Collin needed some DB for desert tonight. I watched Collin through the mirror as I dropped the container in my robe pocket and walked into the living room just as the knock at the door meant dinner had arrived. Collin jumped up and let the waiter in, and they both set up the little table in front of the window.

I poured more wine, took a minute to look out over the river, sipped a little, and watched them in the reflection of the glass. My hand was fondling the magic container, when they both headed for the door. Collin helped the waiter load the cart. With their backs to me now, I looked down at the table to see two beautiful Tiramisu with powdered confectioner's sugar on top---how perfect… I quickly pulled out the container and sprinkled a little white magic on his treat. By the time he returned I was sitting with the top of my robe around my waist, and quite excited, if you get what I mean… he could hardly focus on his dinner. We enjoyed the Chicken Marsalis with a cute portion of cut asparagus, funny though, no salad?

I looked up and asked, "What happened to the salad?"

"I hate salad, it gets in the way of the real food!" Collin remarked as he bit down on a sprig of asparagus.

"Yes Collin, but it's the little things that also need attention, which most men forget!"

"Well put, did you have something in mind that needs my extra attention?"

"Yes, lover---very soon, very soon you will be able to satisfy me fully." Collin began to get up, I had to think fast.

I reached for his desert dish carefully, "Collin, you can't have my treat, until you eat this one." I held it right about nose-level, and leaned in and gave a big blow followed by some laughing just in case it didn't work---but it did, I heard him cough, choke, and sniff. His head fell back for a second as I shoveled a large piece in his month before he could stop me. I smiled and told him to swallow.

Collin dropped his head a little as he chewed, his face was flushed, ears beet red, and when he looked up his devil eyes were blood red and still empty---that hadn't changed. I told him to stand up and unbutton his shirt. Collin did as I told him, I then told him to drop it and undo his pants--- down they fell as I instructed him to kick them across the room. He wasn't wearing any briefs…

I sat and looked him up and down, wondering if all that was as good as it looked. My wonder seemed to be turning to desire. I asked him to walk over here in front of me and kneel. I opened my legs and didn't have to say another word. I will tell you I had my hand on the handle of the letter opener the whole time. And I went off like a Roman candle in record time.

I pushed him away and stared at him sitting there on his knees--- wondering why I just let a serial killer get me off---the only thing I could think of was the fact that he was under my power. He wasn't really the same guy at this moment. I told him to get up and go lie on the bed. I sat and drank, not sipped, my wine, and then poured another, wishing this was Jan's Bash. I could really use a pitcher of her stuff right now.

I have to tell you, I am still a little horny---or is it that I'm just full of anxiety about the next several hours. Rice Crispies, I had no idea as I tugged at my hair, and yes, I walked over to the bed and stepped up on it. I liked being above him and him in my power. Sisterhood came to mind all of a sudden. Well shit, this is for every woman that he over powered, as I lowered myself and went to town like this was his last day on earth---wait, it was his last day on earth, silly me.

After about two hours, I noticed that he must have passed out under me, so I went into the bathroom and slid to the floor and looked out into the bedroom---*what have I done?* My phone was still on the edge of the shower where I left it. I reached for it and dialed Jack. I needed to hear his voice for some reason.

"Raven, it's late, are you ok? Your voice, Raven, why are you whispering?"

"Jack, it's late, I don't really know why I called, something about hearing your voice, something about you working so hard to find my sisters killer I guess."

"Hey, we will find him, and make him pay."

"Tell me how you will make him pay, Jack, with a bullet, hang him from a tree, or jail---which one, Jack?"

Jack had no words for me, just silences. In the quiet, I heard a woman's voice. She must be with Jack. I asked who that was.

"That is Tory, she is the Medical Examiner working with us, Raven."

 "Tell me what she just said!"

"Tory said something in Persian, it roughly meant sisterhood, and that these girls are of a sisterhood now. Tory repeated that over and over. She is right, they all have this in common. They are or were innocent women killed at the hands of a sick individual, and no one has been fighting for them."

"*Sisterhood*, that's it, she is right, Jack, thank you for that---but who is going to give them the justice they deserve? Is the FBI going to do that? I know the answer, Jack---maybe someone will give them the justice they are looking for, the kind they are looking for---maybe someone needs to fight for them."

'Raven, we are doing everything we can do---this is our job and we are getting closer, I promise."

"Wow, a promise." Jack picked up on the change in tone, almost a different voice all together.

I sat there on the floor of the bathroom, listening to Jack trying to make me feel better. There is only one thing, only one thing, that will make me feel better and that is a painful death to a Cock-Spur of a man. The morning can't come soon enough. I watched the flickering light from the blade of the letter opener dance against my face as I watched Collin lay naked on the bed in the next room.

Jack was talking, but I really didn't hear anything he was saying. I studied the blade of the letter opener, and thought how easy it would be to just walk over there and plant it in his forehead, and see him die at my hand. The pain, everyone's pain would fade, that's how it works, right…?

Epilogue

Two Birds with One Stone

'So now it is time to disassemble the parts of the jigsaw puzzle or to piece another one together, for I find that, having come to the end of the story, my life is just beginning!'

Conrad Veidt

"HELP ME, HELP ME GOD, HELP ME!"

About a hundred yards down the Folly Beach shoreline, just outside of Charleston was a woman staggering along the water. I could hear brief whimpering sounds in between the crashing waves as she got closer.

Then suddenly the woman dropped to her knees in the water, and began screaming at the top of her lungs, "I want to die!" as waves overtook her.

I dropped my wine glass in the sand and ran to her. As I reached her, she threw herself face down in the water. I put my arms around from behind, when she began to throw her arms in the air and twist and turn trying to escape. This woman was trying to kill herself! I had to use a bit of force to get her under control and get her to listen to what I was saying.

As we sat there, waist deep in the dark waters of the Atlantic, she just cried and kept asking why, just why---the woman kept repeating herself. I had no idea what this woman was upset about, and she was in no condition to speak rationally. I looked up and down the beach but couldn't see anyone else around.

I was able to drag her up out of the water and walk to the shore. Then I began to steer her up to my bungalow just about fifty feet down the beach. She fought me part of the way, but it wasn't until I wrapped my arms around her tight that she stopped fighting and fell into my embrace. I moved her to my porch and sat her in a chair while I wrapped a towel I had used earlier around her as she just shook." Let me get you some wine to warm you, ok? "

All she could do was nod, yes. I went inside, afraid to leave her alone, but I was alone. I grabbed two glasses while keeping an eye on my guest. Poured as fast as I could, then ran back out to the porch. I placed the wine in her shaking hand, she grabbed it and reached out with her other hand to grab mine to hold on to her. She then tipped up the glass and took it down with one swallow.

Funny, I just did the same thing. I sat my glass down and ran my hands up and down her shoulders trying to warm her, when she lifted her glass and asked for more. I thought "wow," and grabbed the bottle to fill her glass. She reached for it before I was done filling it, and wine spilled out on the table. Before I could set the bottle down, she had taken in the entire glass. I shook my head as I sat next to her and asked if she was ok--- "yes, thank you."

That was all I got, but that was a start. I reached behind me to turn on a little light that sat on the table next to the chair. When she noticed what I was doing, she swung and knocked it off the table and into the sand, then grabbed me and held me so tight I couldn't breathe. I let her shaking body hold on for what seemed like an hour.

"Why does he hate me?" she said.

I paused for a moment before I gently held her face up and asked, "Who hates you, Darling?"

She pushed me back, and said, "My husband!"

The full moon came out from behind the clouds and lit up the sand, casting enough light for me to see that she had black and blue marks on her chin and a busted lip with more bruises under her left eye.

"Do you see my face? This is what happens when he gets upset---upset at football, work, or if I didn't do something the way he demanded."

I guess my face didn't hide how I felt after seeing her face up close. Flashes of Sara and Karl's wife flashed around my head…

I saw now why she didn't want the lamp on. "How long has he been doing this to you?"

"I guess since High School."

I didn't say a word, anything I might say would be wrong. I noticed my left hand starting to shake, like just before a mind orgasm comes over me---I can't let a mind orgasm hit me right now. It will just throw this woman over the edge---an edge she is standing on right now. I was fighting it and kept her talking. My left arm began to flip flop a bit, but I asked if I could step into the bathroom. She smiled and said yes, that she was ok.

As I got up, and I handed her the bottle and pointed at her empty glass, she actually laughed. That was a good sign, right? I hit the bathroom and stood in front of the small mirror, telling myself this was not good now! How can women let this happen over and over again? To beat all, they act like it isn't happening, and go on with life just like you and me. So much for my peace, part of me is thinking to just take her back to the resort and let her go, then---there is that other part, which is saying---no yelling at me to ask more questions.

What is a girl who just murdered a shit bag that preyed on women, to do? If I ask more questions, I am going to get involved, and that may not be good---just look at the past several months with the Collin project. I threw some water on my face and walked back out, half thinking she would be gone. Nope, there she sat seeming a little more at ease.

"So, what's your name by the way? Mine is Raven."

"I'm so sorry you had to find me like this; he just got really bad tonight and I couldn't take it, I had to leave---not really knowing where to go, but I had to leave. My name is Katie, again, I'm very sorry."

I looked down at her, not saying anything, just giving her a half smile. I knew I had to watch what to say next. So, I asked the typical bull shit questions, how do you do stuff and the classic, do you live here. She smiled and told me they were from Miami. Her husband was a car salesman for a foreign exotic car dealership. She went on to tell me that she worked for an IT company that specialized in corporate security. Ok, granted I got her wined up and she is talking, but it sounded like she could hold her own in the work world, so why is it different behind closed bedroom doors?

Katie hadn't stopped talking, she was going on about the company. She had just received a high security clearance, and that they were working on two government projects---one that dealt with data bases for law enforcement, and the other was a military application of some sort. I'm sure she shouldn't be telling me these things, but it seems we are BFF's now.

I had to stop her and get her focused on the problem. She dropped her head and told me, yes, she noticed it back in high school, but she was a geek, and he was so cute. The prince and frog story every girl falls for. Then it was strange she said it, because it became like it was normal---he would hurt me, then beg for forgiveness, telling me he would never do it again. Well, we know it did happen again---again and again.

She did stand up once, told him he would have to get help with his problem. He did---a girlfriend, or fuck buddy, whatever they call it now. Things seemed to get better for her at that point, so she said she threw herself back into her work.

"Raven, I even developed some great software that my company patented, which I share in. Raven, to answer your unasked question--- yes, I do have a separate bank account he knows nothing about. You see I'm making little steps to free myself. I really thought he would leave me once he had the other girl, but for some reason the bastard will not let me go."

"Do you think it might be that he knows he can control you and take his shit out on you---you know, a power thing?"

"Whatever, I just need him gone, gone from my life. I want to feel free and not look over my shoulder every minute and smile at people without being slapped in the mouth and called a slut---after all, he has a slut to do whatever to. I just want him gone."

"Katie, do you want me to give you the name of a good lawyer?"

Silence took over the porch as I watched Katie rock back and forth in her chair. She had a look on her face that I was very familiar with. She wanted him dead, she wanted him to feel the pain and powerlessness of being at the hands of someone else. I could feel the little hairs stand up on the back of my neck, and a tingle between my legs like when I helped Collin solve his woman issues.

"Katie, the boat---your boat is leaving in the morning, right?"

"At 10:30, headed south for the night, then Key West and on to Mexico, why?"

"Well, Katie dear, I was thinking I could join you and meet your husband."

"Raven, what are you saying?"

"I could use a little boat ride to Key West for the night, and, well…kill two birds with one stone---so to speak."

I watched her face lighten up, and I went out on a limb and sat in front of her, took her hands in mine, and asked, "Katie, what if there is a way to free you, and you don't even have to lift a finger?"

"Raven, I don't understand---what is it that you are saying? Please, just tell me what you mean."

I looked into her eyes with mine, the eyes that watched my sister swing in a tree, and told her I would kill him for her, and set her free. She pushed herself back in the chair, not saying a word, but she still had that look in her eyes, and I knew this could go a couple different ways.

"Raven, tell me how you would kill the bastard, and would it hurt?" Not what I thought she would start with, but ok---

"Well, I need to know if you are really in, or just playing, Katie. I'm not playing---well, actually it is playing for me. Katie, if you can't hold up and go through with this, I need to know now. I can take you back to the hotel and we will never see one another again. You can go back to your life of being dominated by a pig and catching a few slaps now and again."

Her grip tightened as she leaned in my face and said, "Kill the fucker. Make him pay for all the busted lips, bruises, broken arm. I want him to pay, pay in pain---will you do that, will you do that for me, Raven?" as tears fell from her face, and her whole body trembled. I knew she was in. I reached for her, hugging my new sister, sisterhood, as it was.

"I have to make a call, let me go and we will put this all together in a minute, ok?" She let go and I went into the bungalow to get my phone.

"Hey, it's me---I need a boarding pass for the Ecstasy 1 departing Charleston in the morning at 10:30. Can you make that happen? I am also going to need a car waiting in key West the next day."

"Anything else, my dear…?" Jean-Paul asked with a sarcastic flare in his voice.

"I think I have it covered."

"Raven, walk me through what you think you are doing. Let me help." I told him that I had met a young woman who almost killed herself due to an abusive husband—a person who I am now going to kill."

"So, you have decided to *'play' again*---very nice, Raven. I will have everything taken care of. Wear the black, black wig and do the white face tomorrow. I will have Brazil pick you up in the morning and put you on the ship. There will be no pass needed, and I will make sure you get a special room. The car will be ready in the Keys. I don't like the whole ship thing though---too many things could go wrong."

"I understand, but I will handle myself just fine---how many people do you have on the ship?"

Laughter filled the phone and he told me, "I have a couple. I have even more in the Keys---that's my Port of entry for the Faksyon, to service the east coast."

"I actually need a balcony for my plan to work."

"I would not have put you in a room of any less luxurious amenities to satisfy even the most discerning traveler. I know my 'Queen of New Orleans' by now—so get back to your guest, and be careful."

Katie was down by the water, standing ankle deep as the small waves washed up. I watched her for moment thinking about the world I just introduced her to. I hope she can handle it. I really hope she can understand it.

"Hey, are you doing ok?" as I went down the steps and met her at the water's edge.

"Raven, life has never been clearer than right now. You have lifted a weight off me, and now I can see what's in front of me. It's funny how free I feel, how strong I feel, do you do this for other women---the *Sisterhood* thing, I mean?"

I have to say, she stopped me in my tracks with that statement. Sisterhood?

Made in the USA
Columbia, SC
23 May 2019